Step into the world of NYC Angels

Looking out over Central Park,
the Angel Mendez Children's Hospital,
affectionately known as Angel's,
is famed throughout America for being at the
forefront of paediatric medicine, with talented
staff who always go that extra mile for their
little patients. Their lives are full of highs,
lows, drama and emotion.

In the city that never sleeps, the life-saving
docs at Angel's Hospital work hard, play hard
and love even harder. There's *always* time for
some sizzling after-hours romance…

And striding the halls of the hospital,
leaving a sea of fluttering hearts behind him,
is the dangerously charismatic new head of
neurosurgery Alejandro Rodriguez. But there's
one woman, paediatrician Layla Woods, who's
left an indelible mark on his no-go-area heart.
Expect their reunion to be explosive!

NYC Angels

*Children's doctors who work hard and love
even harder…in the city that never sleeps!*

Dear Reader

Have you ever known a people-pleaser—someone who will do anything to keep others content? Perhaps you are one. If so, you know what a huge undertaking making everyone happy can be. Impossible, even. Yet Polly Seymour, RN, plods ahead with her challenging life, insisting upon sprinkling seeds of joy everywhere she goes, whether a person wants those seeds of joy tossed their way or not.

On the other hand, we might all also know the proverbial curmudgeon. A person who has been kicked in the teeth by life once too often—someone who has forgotten what it's like to be a part of the huddled masses, yearning for something better. Most observers would give up on him and his sour moods. But someone astute at reading people, like Polly, recognises a man with a big heart even if he doesn't want to admit it. Because any man whose day isn't complete until he's said goodnight to each of his hospitalised paediatric patients can't be all bad, right? Meet Dr John Griffin.

Throw these two most unlikely people together on a busy orthopaedic hospital ward, let them duke it out—her killing him softly with her charm, him coming off gruffer than he intends—and watch the sexual sparks fly. It just goes to show you never know which small gesture or innocent invitation might reach inside another person's heart and start the healing.

Now imagine running into someone your first day on a new job—someone who will change your life—but all you feel is annoyed. Imagine being the newest employee on the ward and still having the nerve to approach the head of the department with a grand idea. Imagine two damaged people, struggling to make it through each day, using completely different coping mechanisms. Meet Polly and John, two people I hope you'll root for as they stumble and fumble their way towards that often elusive prize—their very own happy-ever-after.

Welcome to **NYC Angels**—the hospital that won't turn anyone away.

Happy reading!

Lynne

Lynne Marshall loves to hear from readers. Visit www.lynnemarshall.com or 'friend' her on Facebook.

NYC ANGELS: MAKING THE SURGEON SMILE

BY
LYNNE MARSHALL

Many thanks to Mills & Boon for the opportunity to participate in this wonderful Medical Romance™ continuity.
Special thanks to Flo Nicoll for creating Polly and John, two characters I grew to think of as friends by the end of this book.

First published in Great Britain 2013
Harlequin Mills & Boon Limited,
Eton House, 18-24 Paradise Road, Richmond, Surrey TW9 1SR

© Harlequin Books S.A. 2013

Special thanks and acknowledgment are given to Lynne Marshall for her contribution to the *NYC Angels* series

ISBN: 978 0 263 23363 6

Harlequin Mills & Boon policy is to use papers that are natural, renewable and recyclable products and made from wood grown in sustainable forests. The logging and manufacturing process conform to the legal environmental regulations of the country of origin.

Printed and bound in Great Britain
by CPI Antony Rowe, Chippenham, Wiltshire

Lynne Marshall has been a Registered Nurse in a large California hospital for over twenty-five years. She has now taken the leap to writing full-time, but still volunteers at her local community hospital. After writing the book of her heart in 2000, she discovered the wonderful world of Mills & Boon® Medical Romance™, where she feels the freedom to write the stories she loves. She is happily married, has two fantastic grown children, and a socially challenged rescue dog. Besides her passion for writing Medical Romance™, she loves to travel and read. Thanks to the family dog, she takes long walks every day!

To find out more about Lynne, please visit her website: www.lynnemarshallweb.com

Recent titles by this author:

DR TALL, DARK...AND DANGEROUS?
THE CHRISTMAS BABY BUMP
THE HEART DOCTOR AND THE BABY
THE BOSS AND NURSE ALBRIGHT
TEMPORARY DOCTOR, SURPRISE FATHER

These books are also available in eBook format from www.millsandboon.co.uk

NYC Angels

Children's doctors who work hard and love even harder…
in the city that never sleeps!

Step into the world of NYC Angels and enjoy two new stories a month

In March New York's most notoriously sinful bachelor Jack Carter
found a woman he wanted to spend more than just one night with in
NYC ANGELS: REDEEMING THE PLAYBOY
by Carol Marinelli

And reluctant socialite Eleanor Aston made the gossip headlines
when the paparazzi discovered her baby bombshell
NYC ANGELS: HEIRESS'S BABY SCANDAL
by Janice Lynn

In April cheery physiotherapist Molly Shriver melted the icy barricades
around hotshot surgeon Dan Morris's damaged heart in
NYC ANGELS: UNMASKING DR SERIOUS
by Laura Iding

And Lucy Edwards was finally tempted to let neurosurgeon
Ryan O'Doherty in. But their fragile relationship
had to survive her most difficult revelation yet…
NYC ANGELS: THE WALLFLOWER'S SECRET
by Susan Carlisle

In May, newly single (and strictly off-limits!)
Chloe Jenkins makes it very difficult for drop-dead-gorgeous
Brad Davis to resist temptation…!
NYC ANGELS: FLIRTING WITH DANGER
by Tina Beckett

And after meeting single dad Lewis Jackson, tough-cookie Head Nurse
Scarlet Miller wonders if she's finally met her match…
NYC ANGELS: TEMPTING NURSE SCARLET
by Wendy S. Marcus

Finally join us now, in June, when bubbly new nurse Polly Seymour
is the ray of sunshine brooding doc Johnny Griffin needs in
NYC ANGELS: MAKING THE SURGEON SMILE
by Lynne Marshall

And Alex Rodriguez and Layla Woods come back into each other's
orbit, trying to fool the buzzing hospital grapevine that the spark
between them has died. But can they convince each other?
NYC ANGELS: AN EXPLOSIVE REUNION
by Alison Roberts

**Be captivated by NYC Angels in this new eight-book continuity
from Mills & Boon® Medical Romance™**

**These books are also available in eBook format
from www.millsandboon.co.uk**

CHAPTER ONE

MONDAY MORNING POLLY SEYMOUR dashed into the sparkling marble-tiled lobby of New York's finest pediatric hospital, Angel's. The subway from the lower East
Side to Central Park had taken longer today, and the
last thing she wanted to do was be late on her first day
as a staff RN on the orthopedic ward.

Opting to take the six flights of stairs instead of
fight for a spot in one of the overcrowded elevators,
she took two steps at a time until she reached her floor.
As she climbed, she thought through everything she'd
learned the prior week during general hospital orientation. Main factoid: Angel Mendez Children's Hospital
never turned a child away.

That was a philosophy she could believe in.

Heck, they'd even accepted her, the girl whose aunts
and uncles used to refer to as "Poor Polly". It used to
make her feel like that homely vintage doll, Pitiful Pearl.
But Angel's had welcomed her to their nursing staff
with open arms.

Blasting through the door, completely out of breath,
she barreled onwards, practically running down a man
in a white doctor's coat. Built like a football player, the
rugged man with close-cropped more-silver-than-brown

hair hardly flinched. He caught her by the shoulders and helped her regain her balance.

"Careful, dumpling," he said, sounding like a Clint-Eastwood-style grizzled cowboy.

Mortified, her eyes shot wide open. Sucking in air, she could hardly speak. "Sorry, Dr...." Her gaze shifted from his stern brown eyes to his name badge. "Dr. John Griffin." Oh, man, did that badge also say Orthopedic Department Director? He was her boss.

She knew the routine—first impressions were lasting impressions, and this one would be a doozy. Without giving him another chance to call her "dumpling"—did he think she was thirteen?—she pointed toward the hospital ward and took off, leaving one last "Sorry" floating in her wake.

At the nurses' station, she unwrapped her tightly wound sweater, removed her shoulder bag and plopped them both on the counter. "I'm Polly Seymour. This is my first day. Is Brooke Hawkins here?"

The nonchalant ward clerk with an abundance of tiny braids all pulled back into a ponytail lifted his huge chocolate-colored eyes, gave a forced smile and pointed across the ward. "The tall redhead," he said, barely breaking stride from the lab orders he was entering in the computer.

Gathering her stuff, and still out of breath, Polly made a beeline for the nursing supervisor. Brooke's welcome was warm and friendly, and included a wide smile, which helped settle the mass of butterflies winging through Polly's stomach.

Brooke glanced at her watch. "You must be Polly and you're early. I wasn't expecting you until seven."

"I didn't want to miss the change-of-shift report, and

I don't have a clue where to put my stuff or which phone to clock in on." Would she ever breathe normally again?

"Follow me," Brooke said, heading toward another door, closer to the doctor. "I see you already ran into our department director, Dr. Griffin. Literally," Brooke said, with playful eyes and a wink.

Polly put her hand to the side of her face, shielding her profile from the man several feet away and still watching her. "I think he thought I was a patient."

"Did he smile at you?"

"Yes."

"Then he definitely thought you were one of our patients. He doesn't smile for staff."

An hour later, completely engrossed in taking vital signs in a four-bed ward of squirming children wearing various-sized casts, splints and slings, Polly heard inconsolable crying. She glanced over her shoulder. "What is it, Karen?" The little girl had undergone femoral anteversion to relieve her toeing-in when walking, and was in a big and bulky double-leg cast with a metal bar between them keeping her feet in the exact position in which they needed to be to heal.

Polly rushed to the toddler's crib and lowered one of the side rails. "What is it, honey?"

With her face screwed up so tight her source of tears couldn't be seen, Karen wailed. Polly could have easily done a tonsil check while the child's mouth was wide open, but knew that wasn't the origin of Karen's frustration. She lifted the little one, who weighed a good ten pounds more than she normally would have because of the cast, from the bed and cooed at her then patted her back. "What is it, honey, hmm?"

Perhaps the change in position would be enough to

help settle down the tiny patient. No such luck. Karen's cries increased in volume as she swatted at Polly, who sang a nursery rhyme to her to calm her down. *"Oh, the grand old Duke of York..."* Maybe distraction would work?

"Oh, look! Look!" Polly moved over to the window to gaze out over beautiful Central Park. "Pretty. See?" Praying she could distract Karen for a moment's reprieve, Polly pointed at the lush green trees, many with colorful white and pink blooms still hanging on though late June.

"No!" Karen shook her head and kept crying.

Polly bounced Karen on her hip, as best she could with the toddler's cast, and jaunted around the room with her. "Let's take a horsey ride. Come on. Bumpity, bumpity, bumpity, boom!"

"No boom!" Karen would have nothing to do with Polly's antics.

"I'm going to eat you!" Polly said, digging into Karen's shoulder and playfully nibbling away. "Rror rror rrr."

"No! No eat me."

Felicia, the five-year-old in the corner bed with a full arm cast began to fuss. "I want a horsey ride."

Polly danced over towards Felicia's crib-sized bed, which looked more like a cage for safety's sake. Factoid number two from orientation: hospital policy for anyone five or under. "See, Karen, Felicia wants a horsey ride."

Now both girls were crying, and all the goofy faces and silly songs Polly performed couldn't change the tide of sadness sweeping across the four-bed ward. Erin, in bed C, with her arm in a sling added to the three-part harmony. The only one sleeping was the little patient in bed D, who would surely be awakened by the fuss. What the heck should she do now?

"Hold on," a deep raspy voice said over her shoulder. "This calls for emergency measures."

Polly turned to find Dr. Griffin filling the doorway. He dug in his pocket and fished out a handful of colorful rubber and waved it around. Making a silly face at Karen, he crossed his eyes, stretching his lips and blowing out air that sounded like a distant elephant. Polly tried not to laugh. Quicker than a flash of rainbow he diverted the children's attention by inflating long yellow and green balloons and twisting them into a swan shape. Factoid number three: all balloons must be latex-free. How did he get them to stretch like that?

"Here you go, Karen. Now go and play with your new friend," Dr. Griffin said.

To Polly's amazement, Karen accepted the proffered gift with a smile, albeit a soggy smile in dire need of a tissue.

"Me next!" Felicia reached out her good arm, her fingers making a gimme-gimme gesture.

Dr. Griffin strolled over to her bedside and patted her hand. "What color do you want?"

"Red," she said, practically jumping up and down inside the caged crib while she held onto the safety bars.

"Do you want a fairy crown or a monkey?"

"Both!"

In another few seconds Felicia wore a red crown with a halo hovering above, and gave a squeaky balloon kiss to her new purple monkey friend.

Dr. Griffin glanced at Polly, with victory sparkling in his dark eyes. The charming glance sent a jet of surprise through her chest. Blowing up two more balloons and twisting them into playful objects, he handed one

to the remaining child and left another on the sleeping
girl's bed, then sauntered toward the door. *Was he confident or what?* He stopped beside Polly, who had just
finished putting Karen back into her crib, and blew up
one last balloon. It was a blue sword, and he handed it
to her. "Use this the next time you need to save the day."
He glanced around the room at the quietly contented
children. "That's how it's done," he said.

Polly could have sworn he'd stopped just short of
calling her dumpling again.

He left just as quickly as he'd entered and she paused
in her tracks, feeling a bit silly holding her blue balloon
sword. Outside she heard a child complaining to the
nurse. "I'm sick of practicing walking."

Dr. Griffin joined right in. "I double-dog dare you
to take ten more steps, Richie," he said. "In fact, I'll
race you to that wall."

Was this really the man the staff said never smiled?

Humbled by the gruff doctor's gift with children, Polly
went about her duties giving morning medications and
giving bed baths to three of her four patients. At mid-
morning the play therapist made a visit, relieving her of
both Karen and Felicia for an hour. Erin's mother had
also arrived, which gave Polly one-on-one time with
her sleeping princess, Angelica, the most challenging
patient of all. She had type I osteogenesis imperfecta
and had been admitted for pain control of her hyper-
mobile joints. Her condition also caused partial hearing
loss, which was probably why the three-year-old had
slept through the ruckus earlier.

Thinking twice about waking the peacefully sleeping
toddler, Polly gazed affectionately at her then drifted

to the desk and computer outside the four-bed ward to catch up on her morning charting.

"How are things going?" Darren, a middle-aged nurse with prematurely white hair pulled back into a ponytail, asked. By the faded tattoo on his forearm, she knew he had once been in the navy.

"Pretty good. How about you?"

"Same as always. Work hard, help kids, make decent money, look forward to my days off."

So far Polly wasn't impressed with the general morale of the ward. Everyone seemed efficient enough, skilled in their orthopedic specialties, but, glancing around, there didn't seem to be any excess energy. Or joy. She found it hard to live around gloom, and had learned early on how to create her own joy, for survival's sake. Some way, somehow she'd think of something to lift the ward's spirit, or she wouldn't be able to keep her hard-earned title of professional people pleaser.

A physical therapist came by, assisting one of the teen patients who did battle with a walker. Polly gave a cheerful wave to both of them. The P.T. merely nodded, but the boy was concentrating so hard on his task that he didn't even notice.

Orientation factoid number four: Angel's is the friendliest place in town!

Really?

Polly turned back to Darren. "Can you show me how to work that Hoyer lift? I've got a special patient to be weighed, and I need to change her sheets, too."

"Sure."

"Sweet. Thanks!"

"Now?"

"There's no time like the present, I always say." Polly finished her charting and escorted Darren into her assigned room. Together they gently repositioned and lifted Angelica from the bed. The child stared list-lessly at them, her pretty gray eyes accented by blue-tinged, instead of white, sclera. "Are you from New York, Darren?"

"Yeah, born and raised. Where're you from?"

"Dover, Pennsylvania." She smiled, thinking of her tiny home town. "Our biggest claim to fame was being occupied overnight by the Confederates during the civil war."

Darren smiled, and she saw a new, more relaxed side to his usual military style.

"Don't blink if you ever drive down Main Street, you might miss it." Self-deprecating humor had always paid off, in her experience.

He laughed along with her, and she felt she'd made progress as they finished their task. She could do this. She could whip this ward into shape. Hadn't that al-ways been her specialty? Just give her enough time and maybe the staff would actually talk and joke with each other. She accompanied Darren to the door and sat at the small counter where the laptop was, and prepared for more charting.

"Yo. Whatever your name is." Rafael the ward clerk said, peering over his computer screen. "I've got some new labs for you."

After looking both ways for foot traffic, Polly scooted across the floor on the wheels of her chair in-stead of getting up. "Special delivery for me? Sweet. I love to get mail."

He cast an odd gaze at Polly, as if she were from an-other planet. When he found her lifting her brows and smiling widely, he quit resisting and, though it was half-hearted, offered a suspicious smile back. "Just for you," he said, handing her the pile of reports. "Don't lose 'em."

Brooke came by as Polly perused her patients' labs. "How're things going so far?"

"Great! I really like it here. Of course, it's ten times bigger than the community hospital where I worked the last four years."

"We call it controlled chaos, on good days. I won't tell you what we call it on bad days." The tall woman smiled.

Orientation factoid number five: Teamwork is the key to success at Angel's Hospital.

Hmm. Maybe the staff needed to go through orientation again?

"As long as we all help each other, we should survive, right? Teamwork."

Brooke glanced around the ward, with everyone busily working by themselves, and her mouth twisted. "Sometimes I think we've forgotten that word."

Which put a thought in Polly's mind. As soon as Brooke strolled away, she checked to make sure everything was okay in her assigned room, then went across the ward to a nurse who looked busy and flustered. "Can I help you with anything?"

The woman glanced up from calculating blood glucose on the monitor. "Um." Caught off guard, she had to think, as if no one had ever asked to help her before.

"Anyone need a bedpan or help to the bathroom? I've got some free time."

The woman's honey-colored eyes brightened. She pushed a few strands of black hair away from her face. "As a matter of fact, why don't you ask my broken-pelvis patient in 604 if he needs a bedpan?"

"Sweet," Polly said, noticing a surprised and perplexed expression in the nurse's eyes before she dashed
toward 604.

Polly took her lunch-break with two other nurses and
a respiratory therapist in the employee lounge. They'd
all brought food from home like she had. She'd have to
count her pennies to survive living in New York City.

"Is your hair naturally curly?" One of the other
young nurses asked, as they ate.

Polly slumped her shoulders. "Yes. Drives me nuts
most days."

"Are you kidding? People pay big money to get
waves like that."

"And people pay big money to have their hair
straightened, too," the other nurse chimed in.

"Well, I can't pay big money for anything but rent,"
Polly said. The two nurses and R.T. all grinned and
nodded in agreement. "That's why I stick to my hairband and hope for the best." She thought about her most
uncooperative hair on the planet, and as if that wasn't
curse enough, it was dull blonde. Dishwater blonde as
her aunt used to call it. How many times had she wished
she could afford flashy apricot highlights, or maybe
platinum. Maybe get a high-fashion cut and style to
make her look chic. Only in her dreams. The last thing
she'd ever be described as was chic, and hair coloring
was completely out of the question these days.

She took another bite of her sandwich and noticed
everyone zoning out again. The silence was too remi-
niscent of her childhood, being shipped from one aunt
and uncle to another, and how they'd merely tolerated
her presence out of duty. The sad memories drove her
to start yet another conversation.

"Do you guys ever go out for drinks after work? I mean, I know I just said I'm counting my pennies, but seeing that it's my first day on the ward and all, well, I'd kind of like to get to know everyone a little better. You know, in a more casual setting?"

She saw the familiar gaze of people once again thinking she'd arrived from another universe. "How expensive could a drink or two at happy hour be?" she said. "And wouldn't we miss the rush hour on the subway that way, too?"

"You know, I don't even remember the last time we went out for drinks," the first nurse said, forking a bite of enchilada into her mouth.

"Have we ever gone out for drinks?" the second nurse asked, sipping on a straw in her soft drink can.

"I think once in a while we organize potlucks, but…" The respiratory therapist with a hard-to-pronounce surname on his badge said, scratching his head. "I wouldn't mind a beer after work. What about you guys?"

"That's a great idea," Polly said, making it seem like the R.T. had thought up the plan. "Count me in."

"Where're we going?" Another nurse wandered into the lounge.

"To O'Malley's Pub, a block down the street," the first nurse said. "I hear they've got great chicken hot wings on Monday nights, too. Spread the word."

Well, what do you know, she'd pulled it off. One moment the room had been dead, now somehow she'd managed to infuse some excitement into her co-workers as they made plans to do something different. They smiled and chatted about their favorite beer and mixed drinks, and laughed with each other.

It always felt good to please people. It had been how she'd survived, growing up. She had a long history of perfecting her talent, too. A set of narrowing brown eyes and a raspy voice came to mind. "So who's going to invite Dr. Griffin?"

All went silent again. Polly glanced from face to face to face as they stared at her with varying expressions, all of which implied she'd lost her mind.

"What? You don't invite your department head for drinks?"

The first nurse cleared her throat. "Maybe one of the residents but, uh, he doesn't socialize with us."

"Yeah. He merely tolerates us, and only because he knows he needs us to take care of his patients," the second nurse said.

"But isn't he the guy who approves your raises?"

Three sets of lips pressed into straight lines as they all nodded.

"I dare you to ask him to come along," the nurse who'd just joined them said, as she finished heating her soup in the microwave. She laughed with the others at the ridiculous dare.

"Double-dog dare?" Polly had never heard that expression before Dr. Griffin had said it that morning, but figured now was the right time to use it.

"Triple-dog dare," the last nurse said, taking her place at the table and leaning forward with a clear challenge in her eyes.

Polly knew a set-up when she saw one. Let the new girl hang herself with the boss. Well, she'd seen a different side of him that morning and couldn't believe they'd never seen it too. "How bad can a person be who makes balloon animals for his little patients?"

The four other people in the room looked at each other rather than answer the question. That meant one thing. Polly, the diehard, would have to find out on her own.

As the afternoon stretched on, Polly was surprised by how energized the staff seemed since they'd made plans for after-work drinks.

Even Brooke approved. "This is just the injection of fun we've needed around here. I may have to nickname you Pollyanna."

Polly made her goofy face and shook her head. "Please, don't." Even though that was better by far than being called Poor Polly.

At four o'clock, the first shift of the day had ended and had handed over to the next team. Word had spread about everyone going for drinks at O'Malley's for happy hour, and more than half of the staff had signed on. Some of the evening shift wished they could go, too. Not bad for her first day.

Polly tied her sweater around her waist and licked her lips. "I'll see you all down there in a few minutes."

She'd promised to invite Dr. John Griffin, and she always kept her promises. She walked to the far side of the sixth-floor hospital wing. Staring down the hall at his closed office door, she took a deep breath and strode onward.

Someone knocked at the door. John made a face because it interrupted his train of thought, thoughts he'd been avoiding all day. Just one day. That's all he asked. One day not to remember images from twelve years ago. One day without memories sweeping over him, wrenching his gut. Was it too much to ask for? There was a second knock. "Who is it?"

All he could hear was some whispery childlike sound, but he couldn't make out a single word. Irritated, he raised his voice. "Come in. It's not locked." He tossed his pen across the desk blotter and leaned back in his chair.

Peering around the opening door were big blue eyes. *Those* big blue eyes. Son of a gun, it was dumpling, the young woman he'd mistaken for a teenage patient that morning. Damned if he was going to be the first to speak, he sat watching her enter his office. First her head and shoulders came round the door. Next one foot. Then the other foot cautiously followed suit. There she was, as large than life, except in her case that equaled a petite picture of youth and enthusiasm—the last thing on earth, and especially today, that he needed. When the hell had been the last time he'd actually felt enthusiastic about anything?

With one hand behind her back, she cleared her throat. "Hi, Dr. Griffin."

He sat as still as a boulder. Sure, he'd heard the rumblings about everyone going out for drinks after work that night, and little miss bright eyes being the instigator. Well, he wanted nothing to do with it. He didn't believe in fraternizing with his staff. It didn't set a good example. And even if he changed his mind, today would be the last day of any year he'd choose to break his hard and fast rule.

"Um..." Polly edged closer one tiny step at a time as he stared her down. "A bunch of us are going to O'Malley's for some hot wings and beer, and..." She scratched her nose, her eyes darting around the room to avoid meeting his stare. "Well, I was, um, I mean, *we* were hoping you'd join us."

"And why would I do that?" Even for him it came out gruffer than he'd meant.

She studied her feet. "To help raise your staff's morale?"

"Morale? What's that?"

"When people enjoy coming to work, and work better because of it?" She looked all of fifteen standing there, thick wavy dark blonde hair gathering on her shoulders, saucer-sized eyes, chewing her lower lip, hands behind her back, yet somehow seeming courageous.

Normally, he wasn't into torture, but she'd been the one to come to him. It might be twisted, but making her squirm also distracted him from those morbid thoughts looping over and over in his mind.

"Are you their sacrifice?" he said. She glanced up, looking perplexed. "Did they put you up for the fall, being the new girl and all?"

"No, sir. I *wanted* to invite you. It was my idea."

Her near opaque aqua eyes finally found their mark, and the sight of this young woman staring at him made the hairs on his arms rise. His wife had had eyes exactly like hers. Earlier today, they had been the first feature he'd noticed about the new nurse. Everything else about her physically was completely different from his wife, except those eyes. God, he missed Lisa.

But all the wishing in the world couldn't bring her back.

"Do they need their morale raised?" he said, sounding dead flat even to himself. Who the hell was going to raise his morale? "Don't they have lives to go home to every day? Doesn't that raise their spirits enough without me having to babysit them in a bar, too?"

"They don't need a babysitter. We'd all like to share a drink together, that's all." He saw the pink blush begin on her cheeks and spread rapidly to her neck and ears.

He wasn't a monster. He felt bad that he'd made her feel so uncomfortable, but someone should have warned her about trying to involve him in anything social. Brooke had clearly fallen down on her supervisory duties.

All he wanted to do was go home, hide in a dark room, and bury his sorrow in a glass of perfectly aged Scotch. The world didn't need to know that today would have been Lisa's thirty-sixth birthday. How the hell would it look to be chatting in a bar on a day like this?

"I can't." He stood to signal their meeting was over.

"I double-dog dare you." She grimaced.

He folded his arms and one eyebrow quirked. Was she serious?

With a look of desperation she whipped her arm from behind her back, revealing the silly blue balloon sword he'd made for her earlier. "It's just that I was hoping to buy a drink for the man who saved my day, today. You and that jar of latex-free balloons on your desk."

By the earnest expression on her face he knew it hadn't been easy for her to come into his office and beg him to meet with his staff at a pub. A staff he kept socially at an arm's length yet depended on, no, demanded they give his patients the best medical care in New York. He'd always assumed their paychecks were thanks enough. Maybe dumpling had the right idea.

He didn't have a clue, neither did he care, what would make her need to include him. But the employees were all probably at the bar having a good laugh at the new nurse's expense about how they'd managed to set her up for failure. What a dirty trick. Some nurses really did like to eat their young and this Polly was definitely that. Young. Innocent looking. Fresh. Sweet. Ah, hell, be honest—attractive. He gave a tentative smile. She instantly responded with a bright grin and raised brows, and he was a goner. How could he let someone down with a reputation on the line?

Surely Lisa would understand.

"Okay," he said.

"Sweet!"

"One beer and you're buying."

She nodded, triumph sparkling in her bright blue eyes. "Gladly, sir." She pointed the way to the door with the balloon sword.

"That stays here," he said as he passed her on his way out.

She stifled her giggle when he impaled her with his dead serious stare.

One thing she'd already proved to him. This girl... er...*woman* named Polly was fearless. He liked that.

John had to admit the tall glass of house draft tasted great and felt smooth going down. His newest nurse, in keeping with her promise, had fronted the money to buy it for him, which made it taste all the better. She really wanted him there. When was the last time he'd been wanted anywhere other than in the orthopedic operating room?

The look of surprise on the faces of the group of nurses and techs when he'd walked into the bar had been worth the effort. Everyone had gone quiet for an instant before slowly winding back up to their usual pub noise. He could only imagine what they thought about him showing up, and wondered if anyone had taken bets. He and Polly had shared a quiet but victorious glance.

Chatty Polly had burned his ears on the stroll over, too. She'd practically burst with excitement explaining how much coming to New York and landing a job at such a famous hospital as Angel's had meant to her.

Good for her. The world could use more idealistic nurses. Yet he craved the silence of his apartment, where he could sit in the dark and stare out over the neighborhood—remembering the vacancy where the twin towers used to be, nursing his Scotch, which could never fill the bottomless hole in his heart. Shifting his thoughts to the here and now, he took another drink of his beer and gazed at fresh-faced Polly to help banish the image.

She sat beside him on a barstool, sipping pale ale that left a hint of orange on her breath as she continued to chew his ear. "I wasn't always interested in orthopedics. I saw myself as an emergency nurse." Her eyes went wide. Even in the darkened bar they sparkled. "That is, until I worked my first shift on a busy night with a full moon." She covered her face with long fingers and clear-varnished nails, and shook her head, then quickly peeked up at him. "I thought I was going to die!"

Was everyone this animated, or had he quit noticing? He'd be dead between the ears if he didn't admit she was cute, and likeable. She shrugged out of her sweater and he realized she'd changed her nursing scrubs, which had baby koalas patterned over them, for a clingy pink top that dipped just enough to reveal a full-grown woman's cleavage.

How had he not noticed that all day?

He took another drink and tried his damnedest not to stare. She removed her hairband and put it inside her combination backpack-purse, and those light waves curtained her face in an alluring way, coming to rest on her shoulders...which led his eyes back to her breasts.

He certainly wasn't dead. Just severely inactive.

But this wasn't right, staring down her shirt. He

needed to change his focus. "Bartender, the next round for this group is on me."

Everyone clapped and cheered, even a few people he'd never seen before in his life, and he took another drink of beer, feeling almost human again.

Polly wrapped her arm around his and squeezed. "Thank you!"

"You're welcome," he said, tensing, staring straight ahead, knowing his answer had come out clipped. He hadn't made contact with a woman like this in, well, longer than he cared to admit.

She must have sensed his tension and unwrapped her arm but moved closer on her stool. "So, Dr. Griffin, I've told you all about me, but I don't know where you come from."

The bartender delivered the drinks along the counter, and refilled the bowls with pretzels and mixed nuts.

"I'm a New York native."

"So your whole family is here, too?"

"My parents retired to Florida a few years back, and my sister lives in Rhode Island now."

"Are you married? Do you have any kids?"

If Lisa hadn't been killed he would have been a father of an eleven-year-old by now. But his world had officially ended the day he'd spent digging people out of debris as a first responder on 9/11. His always simmering emotions boiled and he snapped, "Look. I'm here for a drink, like you asked. My personal life is none of your business. You got that?"

A flash of hurt and humiliation accompanied her crumbling smile. One instant she'd been bubbling with life, the next he'd crushed it right out of her. Good going, Johnny. He had no business being around people.

She recovered just as quickly, though, straightening

her shoulders and sticking out her chest, eyes narrowing, as if this routine was nothing new to her. "Sorry for crossing the line, Doctor." She slipped off the bar stool and gathered her things and the glass. "Thanks for the beer." Then she wandered over to a group of nurses a few stools away and joined in with their chatter.

He chugged down the last of his beer, not touching the second glass. "How much do I owe you?" he asked the bartender.

He knew he had no business pretending to be like everyone else. He should never have let the pretty little nurse talk him into it. He was only good for one thing, and that was fixing kids with broken bones.

As for the rest of his life, well, that had officially ended the day his newly pregnant wife had gone to work and died on the twenty-second floor of the twin towers.

CHAPTER TWO

POLLY HAD SPENT the entire subway ride home seething over Dr. Griffin's sour attitude. What had she done to turn him against her? After a little cajoling he'd smiled and agreed to go to the bar with his staff. They'd had a brisk and energizing walk to the pub, enjoying the late afternoon sun and moderate June weather. He'd allowed her to buy him a drink, and he'd even made a grand gesture of buying the next round for everyone else.

All had seemed to go according to plan in the people-pleasing biz.

Then she'd asked about his family and the vault door had clanged shut. It hadn't been mere irritation she'd seen flash in his dark, brooding eyes, it had been fury. Plain and simple.

As she prepared for bed in her tiny rented room on the Lower East Side, where the shared bathroom and kitchen were considered privileges in the five-story walk-up, she couldn't stop thinking how she'd messed up that night. Clearly, she'd overstepped her bounds with Dr. Griffin. But how? Didn't everyone love to talk about themselves and their families? That was, everyone except people like her who had miserable memories of feeling unwanted and unloved, like she'd had since her mother had died when Polly had been only six.

She put her head on the thin pillow and adjusted to the lumpy mattress. Of course! How could she be so blind? The man was miserable with his staff. He didn't like to socialize. She'd dragged him out of his comfort zone and asked him about something very personal— his family—then everything had backfired. Something horrible had happened to that man to make him the way he was. Surely, no one wanted to be that miserable without a good reason.

She had to quit assuming that she was the only person in the world with family issues and that everyone else lived hunky-dory lives. Obviously, Dr. Griffin wasn't happy about his family situation and she'd hit a nerve with her line of questioning. Maybe he'd gone through a messy divorce. Maybe his wife had cheated on him. Who knew? But he'd attacked with vengeance when she'd dared to get too personal.

She'd let down her guard, let him skewer her with his angry retort, then, wounded and hurt, she'd brushed him off and moved on. In her world it was called survival, but he'd seen a flash of her true self the instant before she'd covered it up, just as she'd seen his. Well, touché, Dr. Griffin.

Polly folded her hands behind her head and in the dim light stared at the cracked ceiling and chipped paint—what could she expect from an apartment built before World War I?—and thought harder. Maybe she'd inadvertently hurt him as much as he'd hurt her, and, man, she'd felt his anger slice right through her. John Griffin wasn't a person to be on the bad side of. Somehow she'd have to make up for it.

Her eyes grew heavy from the two beers she'd enjoyed at the pub, but one last thought held out until she acknowledged it so she could drift off to sleep with a good conscience. She owed Dr. John Griffin an apology, and first thing tomorrow morning she'd give it to him.

The next morning at work, Dr. Griffin was nowhere to be found. Polly realized during report that Tuesdays and Thursdays were his scheduled surgery days, and felt a mixture of relief and impatience about getting her apology over and done with. She'd never make the mistake of including her boss in any social event again, even though the staff was already talking about another pub night in two weeks. Something else she noticed today was that everyone smiled at her, which made her feel good and far more a part of the team than she had yesterday. At least she'd succeeded in pleasing some people around here.

Her patient assignment was heavy, and although she only had two patients, each needed a great deal of care. Charley was sixteen and in a private room after he'd taken a header on his skateboard, breaking several bones and his pelvis. Her second patient was in surgery and would arrive later in the day after a short stint in the recovery room. Fifteen-year-old Annabelle would also have a private room, having undergone an above-the-knee transfemoral amputation for localized Ewing sarcoma of the lower part of the right femur.

Polly's heart ached for her patient. She'd already been briefed that a team of social workers, psychologists, occupational and physical therapists, as well as wound-care specialists, would be participating in her recovery. Polly would take care of the nursing portion, and for today it would mostly be post-operative care—basic and important for pain control and maintaining strong vital signs. She'd guard against any post-op complications, such as bleeding or infection, to the best of her ability. Tomorrow the reality of being a teenager with a leg amputation would require help from each and every member of that specially organized medical team.

"Here, Charley." Polly handed a washcloth lathered with soap to her shattered-pelvis patient. "You wash your face, neck and chest. I'll help with your back when you're ready."

She believed in letting patients do as much for themselves as possible. Fortunately, Charley had one good arm, and with the overhead frame with trapeze he could lift himself enough to allow her to change the sheets and replace the sheepskin beneath his hips.

She kept a doubled sheet over his waist to give him privacy as they progressed with his bed bath. "Do you miss school?"

He gave a wry laugh. "I miss my friends."

"How are you going to keep up with your studies while you recover?"

He scrubbed his smooth face and chest with the cloth. "They're going to send out a tutor or something. School's almost out for summer break anyway. What really sucks is I was supposed to start driver's training next month."

"Do people even drive cars in New York?"

"I live in Riverdale."

Polly didn't have a clue where Riverdale was but assumed it was a suburb of the city. She'd never, ever want to attempt driving in New York, where being a pedestrian was risky enough.

She washed his back and changed the linen, keeping casual and friendly banter going. "Have you got a girlfriend?"

"Nah. We broke up."

Uh-oh, here she went again, venturing into personal

information that might cause pain. Would she ever learn her lesson? At least he hadn't bitten her head off like Dr. Griffin had. "I'm sorry to hear that."

"It's okay. All she ever wanted was for me to buy her stuff, anyway."

Whew. "Sometimes teenage girls can be very superficial."

"Dude, tell me about it."

Polly gathered the soiled linen she'd heaped onto the floor and shoved it into the dirty-linen hamper just as the door swung open. "Well, look here, perfect timing. Lunch!"

The tall, bronze and buff dietary worker brought in Charley's lunch tray and placed it on the bedside table. Polly washed her hands and checked to make sure they'd delivered the right diet, with extra protein and calories for the growing and healing boy, then left him alone to eat with the TV on while she got his noontime medicine.

When she returned from her own lunch-break the ward clerk informed her that Annabelle was on her way up from Recovery. Polly rushed to the private room to make sure everything was in order then quickly checked up on Charley, who was fine and playing a video game. She explained she'd be busy for a while but made sure his call light and urinal were within reach in case he needed them.

Just as she exited the room she saw the orderly pull a gurney out of the elevator. At the other end was Dr. Griffin in OR scrubs. It was the first time she'd seen him that day and, taken by surprise, her stomach did a little clutch and jump. Would he still be furious with her?

Focused solely on the task, Dr. Griffin helped get

Annabelle into her room. Polly jumped in. "I'll get this, Dr. Griffin."

He let her take the end of the gurney but followed her into the room. She'd pulled down the covers on the hospital bed and had already padded the bed with a layer of thin bath blanket, an absorbent pad and had topped both with a draw sheet in preparation for her patient. She checked to make sure the IV was in place and had plenty of fluid left in the IV bag. Annabelle was in a deep dream state, most of her right leg was missing and the stump was bandaged thickly and thoroughly.

"Careful," Dr. Griffin warned the orderly as he lowered the side rail on the gurney and prepared to transfer the patient to the bed.

Polly rushed to the other side of the bed, got on her knees on the mattress and leaned over to grab the pull-sheet underneath Annabelle toward her. To her surprise, Dr. Griffin came around to her side of the bed and helped out.

"On the count of three," Polly said, as the orderly prepared to pass the patient over from the gurney while they all tugged her onto the mattress. After she counted, they made a quick and smooth transfer. The patient moaned briefly and her eyes fluttered open, but she quickly went back to sleep.

As the orderly left the room Dr. Griffin gave a rundown of Annabelle's vital signs, a job the recovery nurse usually did over the phone, giving Polly the impression of how important the operation and follow-up care were to this orthopedic surgeon.

He ran down the list of antibiotics and pain-medication orders as Polly listened and adjusted the pillow under Annabelle's head. Next she placed the amputated stump on a pillow, checked the dressing for signs of bleeding or drainage, circling a quarter-sized area with her marker and noting the time, then made sure the Jackson-Pratt drain was in place and with proper suction before pulling up the covers.

Dr. Griffin ran his hand lightly over his patient's forehead, gently removing her OR cap and releasing a blanket of thick and shining brown hair. Such a tender gesture for an angry man.

"I'll check back later," he said, giving Annabelle one last, earnest glance before leaving the room. Polly almost expected him to kiss the girl's forehead from that sincere, loving parent-type look in his eyes.

How could she stay mad at a man like that?

"I'll take good care of her, Doctor," she whispered.

He looked over his shoulder and gave an appreciative nod.

Seeing him in his scrubs, OR cap in place, untied mask hanging around his neck, she realized how fit he was, and that his shoulders and arms were thick with muscle. Where he might look stocky in his doctor's coat, he really wasn't. He was just big and solid. For a man she suspected to be pushing forty, he was in terrific shape, and she allowed herself a second glance as he walked away.

"Hey, Doc G., you haven't signed my cast yet!" Charley called out from the next room.

"I'll sign all three, Charley, my boy," Dr. Griffin replied in a cheerful manner, changing his direction and somber attitude on a dime.

How could a man who was so great with kids be so lacking in people skills? It just didn't make sense.

Soon lost in the care of her newly received patient, and also checking periodically on Charley, the afternoon flew by. Before Polly knew it she was giving report to the next shift and preparing to go home. But she couldn't leave yet. Not before she apologized to Dr. Griffin. She'd promised herself she'd make amends today, and she always kept her promises.

Now that he was back from the OR, she knew where to find him and marched far down the hall toward his office as a new batch of butterflies lined up for duty in her stomach. Refusing to be timid this time, she tapped with firm knuckles on the glass of his office door.

"Come in."

Mustering every last nerve she owned, she entered far more assuredly than she had the previous evening, noting the irony in seeing a huge jar of colorful balloons on the desk of a generally grumpy man.

"Is everything okay with Annabelle?"

"She's doing very well, considering." Polly scratched the nervous tickle above her lip. "I medicated her for pain just before I ended my shift." She glanced around the room, with requisite diplomas and awards lining the gray-painted walls yet not revealing anything personal about the man, and took a long slow breath. "What I came for. Well, what I mean is I came here to, you know, after last night and how I upset you, I, uh, I just wanted to stop in and…well…"

"Apologize?" He'd changed back into his street clothes and white doctor's coat. His eyes were tight and unforgiving as they stared at her impatiently. Had she expected anything less?

"Uh, yes." Why did he make her so annoyingly tongue-tied? "As a matter of fact, I did want to apologize for whatever I did to make you angry last night." Heat flared on her cheeks. Frustrated by how uncomfortable he made her feel and how he offered nothing to ease her distress by sitting there just staring, she bit back the rest of her thoughts—*but you were a jerk about it, and anyone with half a brain could tell I didn't mean any harm by asking about your family. It's normal to want to know such things. Sheesh!*

Adjusting the neck of her scrub top, along with her attitude, and desperate for him to like her, she continued. "I overstepped the mark, practically forcing you to go out with the rest of us, then I thoughtlessly insisted you open up and tell me about your family." She held up her hand before he could growl or get angry with her all over again. "Which I understand, as the new girl on the ward, is none of my business. So, yes, I came to apologize. Profusely."

She sat on the edge of the chair across from his desk before her knees could give out. "And I hope you'll accept it, because I really want to be a part of this orthopedic team. I want to help you with special patients like Annabelle." She stopped short of wringing her hands, choosing to lace her fingers and hold tight instead. "I want to help make your job easier by you not having to worry about the level of care your patients receive. I want to be a top-notch nurse, Dr. Griffin. I want to be that for you, sir." Could she possibly grovel any more?

"Stop it already." He brushed off her apology with a wave of his hand. "I was needlessly sharp with you last night. I should be the one apologizing."

"But I started it, sir."

He gave an exasperated sigh. "Okay. I accept your apology. But knock off the 'sir' baloney and call me what my friends calls me. Johnny."

Stunned by his instruction, she could hardly get her lips to move. "Johnny?" For such a simple name it sounded breathy and foreign, the way she repeated it. How could she call the head of the orthopedic department Johnny? Wasn't that the shortened form for young boys named John? It seemed only families would continue to call a grown man Johnny, yet he said his friends called him that. Was he implying she was now a friend?

"Right. Johnny. Now get out of here. I've got work to do." The terse words fell far short of carrying a punch, in fact they rolled off her back. Maybe she'd really gotten through to him.

"Sweet." She didn't mean to say that out loud and couldn't stop the smile stretching across her lips. "Thank you, Doctor. Uh, I mean, *Johnny.*" She emphasized his name. "Thanks so much." She stood to go, relieved beyond her wildest dreams. How had this mattered so much to her in such a short period of time? She shrugged. All she knew was that her apology and his acceptance of it did matter. "I'll see you tomorrow." *Johnny-boy.*

"Good, because I want you assigned to Annabelle for the rest of the week."

"You do?" He trusted her nursing skills enough to ask her to take care of an extra-special patient. This was definitely progress on their ultra-rocky-start.

"Yes. Now would you please leave, or I'll never get out of here tonight."

Still smiling, she looked him in the eyes. His had softened the tiniest bit, but she could also see a slight change in attitude. Yes, she could. "Yes, sir." When she reached the door, calm washed over her and she turned round. "See you tomorrow, Johnny."

Already back at work, he nodded while writing, rather than look up. "Let's keep that name between you and me."

She'd accept that, too. This desperate need for him to like her would have to stop, but for now she was pretty darned glad she'd fumbled her way through the apology, and wondered how many other employees got to call their boss by their first name, even if only in secret?

John had to admit the sputtering woman on the other side of his desk had been strangely captivating. Perhaps it had to do with the fact that she was easy on the eye, energetic, full of life, and had a nice ass, too. When was the last time he'd noticed something like that? Her earnest and unrehearsed apology had done strange things to a few nerve endings in forgotten parts of his body. Not that he was into dominance and submission, but he really liked her baring it all, as it were, by nearly begging him to forgive her.

Hell, he should be the one apologizing to her. He'd treated her badly and had seen a flash of anger in her eyes, which she'd quickly covered up, and instead of calling him an ass, which he deserved, she'd taken the high road. She'd brushed off his remark with a mere flutter of her eyelashes and moved on.

That showed grit, and he liked grit in a woman.

He reached into a desk drawer, withdrew a bottle of water and took a long draw. Her Pollyanna attitude of be-nice-to-everyone was far from his own style, and probably a cover-up for her insecurities. A wry laugh escaped his lips. Who the hell was he to analyze anyone? His style was more make-nice-to-no-one because he didn't give a damn. But he had to admit she had a special way with kids. And his staff.

Remembering how she'd given a horsey hip-ride to Karen in her clunky cast yesterday morning made John smile. She'd been in way over her head with that group of toddlers so how could he not have gone to save the day? He knew his kids. Knew pediatrics. That was his comfort zone.

Adults were the issue for him. He didn't particularly like most adults, merely tolerated them. He had to get along with them if he wanted to continue to run the orthopedic department, and for the past twelve years his motto had been, Do what you have to do to survive, the kids need you.

How had he survived all these years without his Lisa? He pressed his lips together, allowing one little thought about Polly to slip inside his head. She oozed life, something he'd given up on, yet her vibrant approach to things really appealed to him. Maybe he wasn't as far gone as he'd thought.

Looking around the ward that afternoon, when he'd returned from surgery, he'd seen a more cohesive staff. They had been talking to each other and helping each other, even joking. He'd never seen them so happy.

The question was, had his sour attitude spilled over to his staff, and had this Polly from Pennsylvania saved the day?

Her big blue eyes and trembling lips came to mind. Why had he had the urge to run his thumb over her lips to test how soft they were? More importantly, what was with the impulse he'd had to wrap his hand around the back of her neck and drag her to him to test those lips on his?

When was the last time he'd given a woman permission to call him Johnny? What was up with that? What else might he get her to beg for so he could grant her permission? Most importantly, what in hell were these crazy sexy thoughts she'd planted in his head?

Maybe Pollyanna wasn't nearly as innocent as she let on. *Well, guess what, dumpling, neither am I.*

He guzzled more water and scratched his chest, surprised by his thumping heart. Antsy to finish his work and get the hell out of there, he veered his surprisingly sexed-up thoughts away from Pretty Polly and back to dictating his surgery reports for the day. Before he left he'd check on his kids, each and every one—like he did every day before he went home.

Maybe that was the reason he had been out of sorts yesterday at the bar. Maybe it hadn't been because she'd gotten too nosey, or had threatened his resolve never to feel again, or because he'd wanted to go home and brood, which he had to admit was beginning to get boring, even for him. He'd blame it on not saying goodnight to his kids, because he hadn't been ready to admit he was a man clinging so tightly to his past he'd forgotten how to socialize with the living.

Polly had rushed him away from work and he hadn't had a chance to tell all of his patients goodnight, and things just didn't seem right when he missed saying goodnight to his kids.

Yeah, he'd use that as the excuse for his behavior last night, otherwise he'd seem far too pitiful the next time he looked in the mirror.

CHAPTER THREE

THE NEXT MORNING Polly rode the hospital elevator up to her floor. A vibration in her pocket alerted her that a text message had come through her cell phone: *B in NY in 2 wks. Have dinner with me? Greg*

Rankled, since *Greg* had dumped her for another girl over a year ago, and she'd been heartbroken as well as angry at the time, she wrinkled her nose and shut off her phone with a harrumph.

"Bad news?" A familiar voice came from over her shoulder.

"Oh." She turned round. "Dr. Griffin, I didn't see you there." There were several people she didn't know in the overcrowded elevator but she hadn't noticed him mostly because she had been lost in her thoughts and hadn't been looking at anyone. Aching from her lumpy bed, already dragging from the daily rush to the subway, getting pushed and bumped the entire commute, and now hearing from an unwelcome voice from her past, she couldn't begin to paste on a cheery face today.

John edged closer to her. "You don't look happy."

She lifted a corner of her mouth. "I'm not. Old boyfriend just texted me." What did she care if he discovered that little miss Pollyanna from Pennsylvania was a sham, that her carefree moods were manufactured from hard work and years of practice.

"Sorry to hear that," he said, sounding curiously sincere.

"About the boyfriend or not being happy?"

"Both."

"Really?"

"Don't act so shocked." He gave her a John Griffin style smile, which meant it was hard to differentiate the smile between a grimace and/or gas.

"Do you actually notice things like people's moods?"

"No. Not usually."

What the heck did that mean? Had her self-deprecating plea last night in his office put her on his pity list? Maybe she'd overdone it.

"Well, thanks anyway," she said, lifting her brows and glancing toward the neon numbers indicating the floors, having run out of superficial things to talk about. The elevator stopped and several people got off.

He moved closer and whispered near her ear. "You know, you don't have to put on your forever-cheerful act for me."

Had he seen through her already? "Gee, thanks." She didn't mean to sound disrespectful, but he'd just given her permission to show her true feelings, hadn't he? She glanced to where he stood. There was that gassy grimace-style smile again and a playful glint in his eyes. Why did she find it cute?

Cute? John Griffin?

Maybe it was his mouth, the way the marginally off-center bottom lip curled out ever so slightly, making her want to take it between her teeth and nibble... just a little.

Come on, Polly, the guy is way too old for you. Prob-

*ably pushing forty. And gruff as a bulldog. Who needs
the aggravation?* Besides, there was no way he'd ever
be interested in her. Yet…that goofy attempt at a smile
could only be described as cute. Charming, even.

The elevator came to a stop on the fifth floor and everyone else exited. Once the doors closed, John leaned
his shoulder on the elevator wall and looked directly
at Polly.

"Let's make a deal," he continued to whisper. "I'll
show you mine if you show me yours."

She lifted her head from staring at her scuffed white
clogs with the image of nibbling his lower lip fresh in
her mind. "What in the world are you talking about?"

"Our moods." So he had seen through her carefully
crafted façade.

"Well, no offense, Dr. Griffin, but I think I've already memorized your moods. Moody. Grumpy." She
used her fingers to tick off the list. "Gruff. Did I say
moody?"

What do you know, she'd coaxed out a real smile.
"Yes. Smartass." He squinted graciously under fire, his
dark eyes showing signs of renewed life. "Don't forget
Bashful and Sleepy, if you're thinking of naming all of
the seven dwarfs."

"And Doc. You definitely qualify for that one." She
sighed, realizing that whatever this silly game was she
was playing with *Johnny,* many of her cares had already evaporated in the stuffy elevator. By giving her
the okay to be who she really was, warts and all, he'd
liberated her from being Pollyanna. It felt pretty darned
good. Hmm, had he said bashful? Him?

"Bashful? Not you," she said.

"Oh, yes, I am."

"I don't believe it."

"You'd be surprised."

The elevator door opened and they got out and headed their separate ways, she giving a genuinely bright smile, thanks to his lightening her mood, and he, well, still looking gassy but with an added spring to his step. That on-the-verge-of-flirting look he'd just sent her way was bound to stay in her mind and keep her smiling the rest of the day. The little fizzy feeling that look had given her hadn't been half-bad either.

Dr. John Griffin. Bashful? As in let the woman make the advance? Just what else might she be surprised about with him?

As Polly walked to the nurses' locker room, one more thought popped into her head. Johnny smelled good, too, like expensive aftershave and clean hair. Combine that with his rugged, all-man features and her new interest in the shape and angle of his mouth, thinking it looked all too kissable for a guy with salt-and-pepper hair, for a head of Pediatric Orthopedics, and she lost her step and tripped on the doorframe.

All things considered, Johnny Griffin had done a great job of lifting Polly's spirits that morning.

"How's my girl doing?" John asked Polly, entering the hospital room shortly after she'd taken Annabelle's midday vital signs.

"Great! Thanks," Polly said. "Annabelle's doing really well, too." She caught and enjoyed the quick confusion in his eyes before he got her joke.

"You've got a real smart aleck for a nurse, Annabelle." He took his patient's thin hand, and the gesture squeezed Polly's heart.

Annabelle gave a wan smile, and John lingered over her bed like a fussing papa until she closed her eyes.

Polly had given her pain medication through a shot into the hip a few short moments ago.

"The nurses told me she'd had a rough night, complaining about phantom pains, and when she started mentioning them again just now, well, I wanted to make sure she was extra-comfortable today."

He folded his arms across his broad chest. "Good. We'll give her some rest now, but by later this afternoon I want her out of bed and in a chair for at least an hour."

"Got it."

"Physical therapy will start tomorrow, and the wound-care specialist should pay a visit this evening when her parents are here to discuss dressing changes when she goes home."

"Yes, sir."

"You can knock that stuff off, too."

"You don't want me to follow your orders, sir?" Why did teasing her superior feel so delicious?

He took a deep breath, as if trying to suck in patience from the room air. "Are you trying to bug me?"

"Am I doing a good job...sir?"

"Very."

"Good," she said, straightening out the bedspread and double-checking the IV rate. She didn't dare look over her shoulder, but she sensed he was enjoying her feisty mood. Would any of his staff ever dare to give him a hard time?

"There's no excess drainage from the surgical site, and I emptied thirty ccs from the drain at the beginning of my shift," she said, all business.

He checked under the recently smoothed covers and found the Jackson-Pratt bulb was nearly empty. The quarter-sized marking on the post-op dressing hadn't gotten much bigger either, as he soon noticed.

"Good." He lingered at the bedside.

She'd decided, after her pitiful, stumbling apology, and especially their ride in the elevator, that he was a good guy, even if he didn't know it. He'd had the patience of a saint while she'd fumbled her way through her monologue, and he'd rewarded her by telling her to call him *Johnny.* Who else on the staff got to call him Johnny? Not that she ever would, at least not in front of anyone else, especially as he'd asked her to keep it to herself.

"Hey, Johnny." Another doctor entered the room.

So much for the short-lived "special person privilege" fantasy.

"Dave. Come to admire your work?"

"Sure did."

Polly surreptitiously read the other doctor's badge. David Winters. Vascular Surgery. Of course, with the amputation they'd have to make sure the stump had proper circulation, and who better to assist the orthopedic surgeon than a vascular surgeon?

"I was going to wait until later to change the dressing, but there's no time like the present. Polly, can you bring some gauze, dressings, four by fours and paper tape?"

"Sure. Would you like me to bring the Doppler too?"

"Great idea," Dave said.

She knew it was never too early to make sure there was proper circulation to the wound, and the Doppler would let them hear the blood flowing through Annabelle's vessels. A lot rested on every step of the recovery. In order to have Annabelle fit for a prosthetic device she'd need to have a strong and healthy stump. The post op-team, including Polly, would do everything in their power to make sure of Annabelle's success.

After dropping off the supplies, Polly took a quick look at Annabelle's surgical wound as John had already removed the dressing, and was surprised how clean and healthy the skin flap already looked. Cancer of the bone was a curse, but at least Annabelle would be able to wear one of the state-of-the-art prostheses being created these days. One day, when she was back on her feet and used to everything, wearing slacks or jeans, secure in her gait, no one would ever know that part of her leg was missing.

Later that day Polly took Charley his pills. She noticed the three signatures John Griffin had left on the teenager's casts, which made her grin. They were big, just like him, and colorful, hmm, and he had much nicer handwriting than she'd ever imagined any doctor could.

"What's so funny?" Charley asked.

"Nothing. I was just admiring your autographs from Dr. Griffin."

"He's cool."

"Really? He seems so stern all the time."

"Nah, he's funny. And he's the only person who hasn't given me a lecture about my skateboarding."

"Well, I guess accidents do happen, but maybe you should be more careful so as not to tempt the fates."

"Yeah, I get it. And I've heard that before, but yolo, you know?"

"Yolo?"

"You only live once."

So said a sixteen-year-old. "True, but preferably longer than shorter. Right?"

Charley blew her off with a toss of his long-hair. She needed to change the subject back to something lighter, something more interesting for both of them.

"I never would have pegged Dr. Griffin as funny."

"No? You should see him do his Aquaman drowning imitation. And he can sing like that weird guy who got kicked off that TV *talent show* last season, too."

"Are we talking about the same doctor?"

"Definitely. He's a laugh all right."

"Never in a million years would I have thought Dr. Griffin was funny or talented. I mean, the man seems to take himself far too seriously, in my opinion." A second too late, she saw Charley's eyes go wide.

"Is that so?" Johnny Griffin's familiar voice flowed over her shoulder.

"Oh! Hey. We were just talking about you." Heat rushed to her cheeks.

"So I heard."

"I'm afraid you're going to have to do your Aquaman impersonation for me before I believe Charley here."

Charley smiled and, amazingly, so did Johnny-boy. A look passed between them like a secret handshake.

"Stop by my office after work and I'll be glad to give you the whole routine," he said, sounding as though he might be flirting. Really? In front of a patient?

She pointed at him. "I'm tempted to call your bluff on that, Doctor."

"I dare you," he said, a playful, sparkly glint in his otherwise dead-serious eyes. Eyes that were becoming more and more intriguing each time she dared to look into them.

The rock-steady gaze caused a response that zipped down her spine with a surprise destination. What was going on here?

She wasn't sure, but one thing she was positive about, she needed to leave the patient's room before Dr. Griffin got an inkling of how much he'd just excited her.

* * *

Polly's cell phone rang during lunch the next day and she was surprised to see who was calling. It was Greg. She hadn't responded to his text from yesterday. Why the persistence all of a sudden?

"What's up, Greg?" She tried to sound nonchalant.

"Did you get my text?"

"Oh, uh, I've been working a lot. I guess I missed it." She wasn't above lying to someone who'd lied to her. Repeatedly.

He went into his spiel about coming to New York in two weeks and how he hoped to take her out to dinner and maybe even to see a Broadway play. This couldn't be the Greg she'd once known. Would he actually want to take her to an expensive play on Broadway? Not likely. Unless he'd finally come to his senses about what a prize she was. Again, not likely. Maybe he thought he could come to New York on business and cheat on his girlfriend with *her* while he was here? As in letting history repeat itself.

She wouldn't put a sleazy plan like that past him.

One thing was sure—she wouldn't have to find out if she didn't accept his invitation.

"Can you give me a couple days to think this over, Greg?"

"Look, I understand I treated you pretty rotten last year, but I'd really like to see you again."

"Give me a couple days, okay?"

She hung up before he could say another word, desperate to talk over this invitation with someone else. Her best friend back home worked the evening shift and Polly didn't feel comfortable yet about opening up to anyone on staff about her personal issues.

She ate her lunch in silence, deep in thought, then

as she took a bite of her tuna fish sandwich she practically fell out of her chair when one person popped into her head. Johnny. He was the one person on staff she'd made a complete fool out of herself in front of. Now she'd advanced to being able to tell him exactly what she thought and how she felt, even in front of patients and other staff members, much to everyone's surprise. Hadn't he invited her to show him hers if he could show her his in the moody moods department?

She'd tested the waters and had had a great time being completely herself around him the last couple of days, and he had invited her to come to his office after work for the Aquaman imitation. She understood he had only put that invitation out there because of Charley listening in, but still.

Besides, the man had to be a good twelve or so years older than her twenty-seven, and there was no way on earth he'd ever be interested in her. So that wouldn't be an issue. Even if that look he'd given her yesterday had confused her and turned her on.

John seemed level-headed and world-weary. Why not run her dilemma by him? As a guy, he'd have good input for her. It might help her figure out Greg's true intentions, though she had her own strong suspicions. She'd bought herself two days before she had to get back to Greg.

Maybe Johnny could help her see things how they really were. Now, if she could only work up the nerve to approach him.

On Friday evening, for the third time in a week, a light tapping on John's office door interrupted his concentration on the computer. "Come in."

The best thing he'd seen all afternoon, well, since

the last time he'd seen her anyway, which had been two days ago, walked in.

Polly wore black, straight-leg jeans and high wedge heeled shoes with open toes. Red toenails seemed to smile up at him. Her bright blue top clung to her body in soft folds and outlined her breasts and curves in an inviting way. Since when had he noticed what a woman wore, or how much he liked it?

"Finally came to see my Aquaman imitation, did you?" He pretended not to be distracted by how fantastic she looked.

She smiled, a look that spread like warm butter across her face. "Not really."

"What are you still doing here?" he asked.

"I was going to see a movie tonight, and needed to hang around until eight."

She brushed her bangs across her forehead. The rest of her hair hung loose and free, something he hadn't gotten to see while she was on duty or since the bar on Monday night. The waves and curls accentuated her features, big eyes, straight nose, those well-shaped lips, forcing him to realize she was pretty. Damn, she was pretty. "I was just going to pick up some pizza, wondered if you'd like me to bring you a piece, as you're obviously still here at six-thirty."

The thought of pizza did sound good, but if she expected him to join her in the employee lounge, she had another thought coming. "You deliver, too?"

"Sure, if that's what you want."

What he wanted. Well, the picture of youth and suppleness in front of him gave a whole new meaning to what he wanted. Polly had started a domino effect of interest, attraction, challenge, and all-out lust since her arrival this week. He'd spent more time in the last five days missing and thinking about the wonders of sex than he had in all the years since Lisa's death. It wasn't right, but he couldn't stop himself.

For whatever reason, Polly had the right combination of charm and good looks to make his body involuntarily take notice. The thought was wrong on so many levels yet he couldn't give it up. She worked for him, for crying out loud, and what about Lisa? Well, that was a whole other matter.

Maybe having a piece of pizza with the new nurse and having his little fantasy of making love to her might add some long-overdue entertainment. That wouldn't be such a bad way to spend an evening, would it? Compared to his usual Friday nights, a tasty slice of pie and a few naughty daydreams about the new nurse would be a welcomed change.

"You'd actually bring me a couple of slices of pizza, no strings attached?" He could think of a couple of strings he'd like to attach to a place or two on Polly, but that would be wrong on so many levels.

"Sure."

"You're too nice for your own damn good, Pollyanna."

"What goes around comes around, right?"

"That's only when the world makes sense, and most of the time there's no rhyme or reason about what's going on in the world." Especially now with these crazy thoughts about Polly, which seemed to be growing stronger by the minute. Man, he needed to get a grip.

"Are we talking pizza or philosophy?"

He smiled, letting her youthful beauty warm up his innards and tease at that other kind of appetite he couldn't shake. "Maybe a little of both." He sat back in his chair and put his hands behind his head. Was right now one of those life moments a guy was supposed to grab with gusto, or was he going off the deep end? "Can I ask you a question?"

"Of course."

"Why don't I scare you off like I do everyone else on the staff?"

She smiled, took a few more steps toward his desk, and perched on the edge of the chair. He liked the way she kept her knees together when she sat, all prim and uptight. He liked the scent of whatever she'd splashed on her skin after work, too. "It takes a lot to scare me off." She went silent for a moment. "You want the truth?"

Did he really want to find out how a needy people-pleaser like Polly had become that way? It could ruin this perfect storm of a fantasy brewing in his mind. He glanced at Polly, so appealing and open. He needed to quit thinking only about himself. "Nothing but the truth. Lay it on me."

"My mom died when I was six and my dad couldn't handle it. He took off without me. Later we heard he'd been killed in a car crash. After that I got shipped from one aunt or uncle to another. None of them re-ally wanted me, though they pretended they did. Even a kid can tell when someone isn't being sincere, you know?" She gave a wry, lopsided and totally appeal-ing smile. "So it takes a lot more than what you dish out to scare me off."

Her story snuck around his chest like a vine and tan-gled up his already confused feelings. It messed with those more basic thoughts floating around in his head, too. She'd been kicked in the teeth, and she'd gotten used to jerks like him giving everyone a hard time. It didn't settle well on his conscience that, in her world, he was one of the bad guys. Why did one person get kicked in the gut and become unbearable, while another learned to be sweetness and light. Exactly what kind of a heel had he turned into since 9/11?

He had a sudden need to make up for all the times he'd been an ass to her. As hard as it would be, he'd banish those sexual thoughts she kept stoking in his head and show Polly some long-overdue respect. "I've got an idea. Why don't you let me buy you dinner? I know a great Italian joint round the corner."

"Oh, I couldn't let you do that."

"But you will." He stood, took off and hung up his doctor's coat on the rack behind his desk, and walked towards Polly. "Let's go eat. I promise to have you back in time for your movie."

She stood and looked at her backpack and lunch container, and the small plastic bag with her soiled scrubs.

"Leave that stuff here," he said. "You can pick it up later. I promise to get you back in time for your movie. Besides, I've got to come back to say goodnight to the kids."

Her widened eyes showcasing those baby blues looked as though they were calculating a gazillion reasons why she shouldn't let him take over her dinner plans, yet she stood mute. If she'd had any clue how she turned him on, looking at him like that, she would run for cover.

Wondering how long he could keep his poker face, he took her elbow and nudged her along. "Come on, come on, let's go, I'm hungry." He'd use being gruff as his cover, because right now the feel of her skin beneath his fingers set off a whole new list of thoughts he hadn't dared to think in ages.

She lifted her brows higher, which seemed impossible, as if she'd felt something in his touch, too. "Okay, Johnny."

The Italian restaurant named Giovanni's was less than two blocks away, and though Polly's wedge heels weren't exactly made for walking—she'd planned to change into flats before heading for the subway home—she enjoyed the exercise. Being in a big, noisy, polluted city, surrounded by skyscrapers and cement—albeit with many well-kept neighborhood parks, not to mention Central Park to soften the blow—made her miss home. John looked after her as they juggled their way through the passing crowds, ignored crossing lights, and jaywalked to their destination.

Giovanni's was everything she'd hoped for in a restaurant—quaint, quiet, romantic, with tall, thin breadsticks waiting at each table and a handsome young waiter ready and willing to serve the diners. For a Friday night, the place was half-empty, and Polly wondered if it had anything to do with the food. Or if the time being only six-thirty in the city that never slept might have something to do with the small turnout.

Johnny knew the waiter by name and ordered a bottle of Chianti and a medium cheese pizza plus two dinner salads, without giving Polly a chance to change her mind about pizza for dinner. The list of pastas and seafood was impressive, but she had said she was going out for pizza, so she didn't fault him for that. She even kind of liked John's take-charge approach to all things in life.

While in his office she could have sworn there had been a flash or two of something in his eyes, after he'd ordered he gazed at Polly as if noticing her for the first time that day. That interesting curl of his lip stretched into a regular smile, like he was surprised and happy at what he'd found sitting across from him.

"I'm going to be straight with you and say I like your hair down," he said, shaking out his napkin and putting it on his lap, sounding more like he was reading the first order of business at an admin meeting than paying her a compliment.

"Thank you." A warm flush moved in a wave up her neck to her cheeks. Polly couldn't exactly say the sensation was unpleasant, and by the appreciative glint in his eyes he must have found her turning red appealing, which made her face heat up even more.

She'd noticed a few things about him on their walk over, too. Like the fact that he filled out his slacks really well and his broad back made even a man of his size look like he had narrow hips. He walked like a guy on a mission, too, which made it extra-hard to keep up, especially dodging traffic and crossing streets in her wedge-heeled shoes.

The Chianti came quickly, and after downing half a glass of her ice water Polly looked forward to sharing a glass of wine with her boss.

"So," he said, crossing his hands on the table top. "How did your first week at Angel's go?"

"Really well, thank you."

He nodded then took a long draw on his wine, all the while staring into her eyes. He seemed to hold the wine in his mouth before swallowing, as if savoring the flavor and aroma. Oddly, his sensual care with the wine set off tingles across her shoulders. He soon diverted his stare over her shoulder and, she assumed, through the window to the busy street.

"I've got to say, I'm rusty with this sort of thing," he said.

"What sort of thing?"

"Taking a woman out to eat."

Dr. John Griffin didn't date? Even with his gruff shell, that surprised her. He was a good-looking man, a doctor with a gentle heart for his young patients, a... well, she wasn't sure what else he had to offer, but she'd figured he had a full life.

"Don't think twice about it. I practically forced you to do it, so..."

He hushed her by putting his hand on top of hers, and with a no-one-forces-me-to-do-anything look stared her down. "I wanted to."

His touch sent her reeling, and though she thought she might jump out of her seat, she settled and went all quiet, taking in the full significance of his message. Why would he want to spend time with her? She was a country bumpkin, a girl still searching for herself. Sometimes it was better to drop all the questions and just be polite. "Thank you, Doctor."

He shook his head. "Knock off the 'doctor' nonsense. We left that back at Angel's, okay?"

"Okay," she said, as she took her first sip of the strongly flavored wine. "Johnny."

That got an interesting look out of him, one that made her replay her earlier blush.

Midway into her second piece of pizza she'd finished her wine and let John pour her another glass. Another sip or two later, plus more pizza, and she remembered what had really been on her mind since earlier in the week, and why she'd gone to John Griffin's office in the first place.

"May I run something by you?" she said.

"Sure." His mouth was full of the best pizza Polly had tasted since she'd gotten to New York.

She took another drink of wine and placed the glass on the sparkling white tablecloth. "I'm in a dilemma about something and don't know what to do."

He, swallowed, looking very interested in her line of conversation. "Go on."

"I've had a bad history of men walking all over me and, well, last year I got dumped by a guy back home. I'd really had it with men after that, and part of the reason I moved to New York was to move on and start a whole new life."

She could read his body language. Shoulders hunched over the table, his chewing had slowed down. He squinted. This was not a topic of conversation he was interested in but she needed to discuss her options with someone, and tonight that someone was John Griffin.

"So, anyway, a couple of days ago I got a call from Greg, the guy who dumped me without warning last year. He's coming to town and wants to take me out to dinner. He doesn't mean anything to me any more, but I'm thinking he at least owes me a nice dinner, plus he mentioned something about taking me to a Broadway play, too. I know it may sound superficial of me, but I was thinking I deserved some kind of explanation and maybe he'd tell me what was up last year."

He sat perfectly still, hands fisted on the table for a few silent seconds, his expression impossible to read. "He wants to screw you," Johnny said curtly, before taking another drink of wine.

She winced from what felt like a slap in the face. "You don't think I should see him?"

"That depends if you want to get screwed or not." His irritated gaze delved into hers, sending a crazy mixed-up message right down her center. Had she just annoyed him? She sat straighter, using the table to help her balance. Did she want to have sex with her ex? Had she even thought about it in the last six months?

No.

Not until the last few days, that was…and Greg wasn't the face to come to mind when she did think about sex. Oh, cripes, could Dr. Griffin read her mind? Did he have any idea she had the hots for him?

"I'm sorry," she said, putting her napkin across her plate. "I should never have brought up the subject. It's just that I don't have anyone to talk things over with. The lady I rent a room from is probably eighty if she's a day, and my best friend works evenings in Pennsylvania, so it's not like I can pick up the phone after work and talk."

"You asked my opinion." He tugged on his earlobe. "I'm giving it to you straight," he said, his eyes darting around the room in an agitated way. "Unless you want to have sex with the jerk who dropped you last year, don't go near him." He looked at her as if she needed to have a psych referral.

"You're right. I was leaning in that direction, too," she said, mostly to her plate. "I won't even call him back or text him. Thanks for helping me see that more clearly."

Polly sensed a change in John's suddenly irritated mood when she spoke those last words. He inhaled subtly and took another drink from his wineglass, then glanced at his watch.

"We should probably get you back to the hospital to pick up your stuff so you'll have time to get to that movie," he said.

She lifted her chin and gave an exaggerated nod. "Right." She'd blown it. A perfectly lovely dinner with her boss. Until she'd opened her big mouth about some other guy. Could John be jealous? Of course not.

The walk back to the hospital was quiet between them, but the streets, which had come to life with people heading out for the Friday night, weren't. Across the way, Central Park looked hauntingly beautiful in the twilight. John strode on, not saying a word, hands in his pockets, a man on a mission. She did her best to keep up, but her feet were killing her.

"Thank you for buying dinner, Johnny," she said, the only words she could think of. Hoping to remind him he'd given her permission to call him that.

"Any time, dumpling."

That got a smile out of her. He was a paradox. She'd been around many gruff men in her life, but had never cared what they'd thought before. Staring at his profile in the dimming light, she saw a proud man, a talented surgeon, a man respected, if not liked by his peers, yet a man loved by his patients. A man she suspected hid something awful behind his gruff demeanor. Truth was, she found him more and more intriguing and attractive by the moment.

Beginning on Monday, she'd steer clear of him, especially after making a fool of herself by asking him for relationship advice. Whatever had made her think that was a good idea?

Since there was no way in hell she'd ever have a chance with a man like Johnny Griffin, what was the point of being around him? Because she liked him? Found him sexy? The thoughts caused her to pause on the pavement.

That's when he reached for her hand, wrapping his long, strong fingers around it, and pulled her brusquely along the crowded street toward Angel's.

CHAPTER FOUR

POLLY TAGGED ALONG behind John at a fast and challenging clip. They rushed through the hospital lobby towards
the elevator, past the "welcome" clown pacing on stilts
and the piano player, who was smack in the middle of
"Old MacDonald". Diverse entertainment for visiting
hours. He moved like a man with a single thought on
his mind—how to dump his dinner date. Yet he never
let go of her hand.

Still not saying a word on the crowded elevator trip to
the sixth floor, he tugged her down the hall and, having
left his office door unlocked, whisked it open, practically dragging her inside. Only then did he release his
grip. She went directly for her bags and personal items,
assuming he wanted her gone. Now.

Why had she thought that offering John Griffin pizza
was a good ice-breaker in order to bring up her question
about whether or not to go out with an old boyfriend?
All she'd done had been to tick him off.

He stood off to the side, staring out the window,
hands crammed into the pockets of his slacks, looking
like he was doing battle with a slew of demons in his
head. Had she done that to him?

"I feel like you're mad at me," she said, stating the
unmistakable.

He turned abruptly. "I'm not mad at you, I'm angry about how you try to please everyone else and overlook yourself."

She bunched her hands into fists. "I've had a lifetime of practice. Old habits die hard, you know?"

He tugged his earlobe. "I know."

Relieved that he wasn't fuming at her but was more irritated at her situation, a wave of mismatched feelings swept deep, causing confusion in her mind and her eyes to water. She glanced away.

"If you don't mind—" her voice sounded congested "—I'll change out of these shoes for the subway first."

He turned and watched as she sat on the edge of a chair. "I thought you were going to the movies." The man had gone tighter than a stretched rubber band and the muscle at his jaw twitched as he blatantly ground his molars.

"It was a comedy, and I'm kind of not in the mood now."

He cleared his throat. "Sorry."

"It isn't because of you." She slipped off one shoe. "I guess I just realized how tired I am. It's been a long day." She stretched out her foot and toes. "A long week."

His gaze jumped all over her, from her face to her chest to her hips and legs and finally to her foot. His expression changed from indecision and caution to longing and oh-what-the-hell. Something had snapped in him, some decision Polly wasn't privileged to know, yet his change was as plain as the sudden jangled nerves in her stomach. He made an abrupt move, came in front of her and dropped to his knees. Without a word he handed her his handkerchief for her teary eyes then removed her other shoe. His warm, strong hands caressed her foot, sending shockwaves through her.

Polly stiffened as the idea registered of John Griffin giving her a foot massage. She inhaled raggedly while he gently worked the ball of her foot and the arch with amazingly talented fingers. Soothing sensations tiptoed up her calf, causing tingles behind her knee.

Oh, my God, what do I do?

A crazy answer popped into her mind as she wiped away the tears from her eyes with his monogramed handkerchief. *Enjoy it.*

He splayed her toes and worked each joint right out to the tips of her nails. She tensed and sighed, and felt his touch all the way up the insides of her thighs, though his hands never left her foot.

"The problem with women these days," he said, increasing the pressure on her heel, "is they mess up their feet with these super-sexy shoes. All men want to do is get them off." She looked down at his short-cropped, silver-salted hair, discovering a small endearing cowlick in the middle. His voice sounded hoarse, strained, like maybe he really *was* mad at her. Yet his hands told a completely different story. Was he turned on? "I say that as an orthopedic surgeon."

That made her smile, his rubbing her feet in such a sexy way yet trying to pull off a professional manner. He was looking out for her well-being, though, wasn't he? His ministrations were so amazing she couldn't help but sigh again, so he reached for her other foot. Call her easy, but her shoulders slumped and her head dropped back, savoring the heat of his hands on her totally susceptible skin.

"You're too kind to me," she whispered, shifting her gaze from the ceiling to his serious face as he concentrated on the task at hand—her foot. Her incredibly

lucky foot. Her mind wandered to what it would be like
if his hands touched her everywhere like that.

"This isn't about being 'kind' and you know it." He
stopped his massage and delved into her eyes as if measuring the level of her understanding. She concentrated
on his mouth and the hair-thin scar above his upper lip
on the right. The growing warmth between her thighs
weakened when he stopped touching her, but she'd read
his message loud and clear.

He wanted her.

Just as much as she wanted him.

At some point, as he'd stood by that window, he'd
made a decision. She'd sensed it then and felt it with
every fiber now. Saw it in the serious dark eyes staring at her. Whatever he'd needed to overcome, he had,
and now…he wanted her.

A deep desire to break out of her usual by-the-rules
role and not to let this magical moment pass made her
lean towards him, take his life-weary face between her
hands and press a kiss to his irresistible mouth.

Surprisingly soft, his lips were warm and responsive,
and he soon took over the advance, proving her hunch
had been right. He needed her as much as she wanted
him. His hands clamped around her waist, squeezing
with urgency as he deepened their kiss.

She ran her fingers across his short, springy hair then
down his powerful neck as she kissed him back. Solid.
The man was solid. She smelled his lingering forest-
scented cologne and enjoyed the end-of-day stubble of
his beard. His tongue found hers and she let him have
his will, matching exploration for exploration and tasting a hint of Chianti. The warmth pooling between her
thighs quickly renewed as her pulse thrummed throughout her body.

A sharp knocking on the office door shocked her out of her dream about kissing her boss. Oh, wait, it was really happening.

"Environmental Services," a loud voice called. "Dr. Griffin, are you still in there?"

"Just leaving, Constantine, give me a couple of minutes." His voice sounded heavy and forced. Heat radiated from John's darkened eyes as he stared at her. "I know a place we can go. Will you come with me?"

The question of the day—will you come with me?

Overcome with his no-nonsense sex appeal, his smoldering gaze, and their incredible kiss, there was only one answer she could think of.

"Yes, Johnny," she whispered, banishing from her mind their age difference and concentrating on their total attraction to each other.

He hastily gathered her things as she used the back of her hand to wipe her already kiss-swollen lips, trying her best to recover from the mind-bending introduction to making out with Dr. John Griffin. She could barely wait for more as he grabbed his jacket and her hand and led the way out.

"Goodnight," he said in a clipped voice to the janitor as they passed, as if he dragged a woman from his office every night of the week and Housekeeping should think nothing of it.

Was the fact that she was barefoot a dead giveaway to what they'd been doing?

The janitor had his back to them, concentrating on his cleaning cart, and she was grateful as John whisked her down the dark hall toward the stairs.

He led her through the back way and down a couple of flights to another deserted floor, then past half a dozen doors to an open on-call room. Rushing her inside, he hung up the "occupied" sign and closed the door behind them. Immediately, he dropped all of her bags and items into a chair and took her by the shoulders, walking her backwards against the wall.

"Where did we leave off?" he asked gruffly, digging his fingers into her hair before taking her mouth again.

His kisses were hot and wet and making her dizzy with desire. She bunched his shirt in tight fists, wanting him as much as he obviously wanted her. His hand wandered over her hip, skimming her waist and upwards until he found her breast. His other hand cupped her bottom and pulled her flush to his groin. She could already feel his arousal straining against her thigh. Knowing how she affected him excited her beyond any fantasy.

His kisses grew frantic and desperate, and his fingers found their way under her bra. Her breast was already tensed and peaked and he ran his thumb over the tip, which tightened her more. Tingles fanned across her chest, teasing her other breast. She angled the V of her thighs over his erection, and leaned hard into him, yearning for relief. He moaned and pulled her up, positioning her on top of his wedge. She slid over him, begging for more, hating the fact that they were still dressed.

Breaking apart only because she wanted to be without barriers, she raised her arms and he lifted her top over her head in record time. She reached behind and undid the catch on her bra as he unzipped his pants.

"Should we be doing this?" she asked, her eyes adjusting to the darkened room, seeing him stripping in front of her and realizing there was no turning back. Not for her, anyway.

"You started it." He kicked off his loafers and

dropped his pants. Thickly muscled legs, like those of a Grecian god, made her gasp inwardly.

"I didn't think it would get this far." Impatient to be skin to skin with him, she moved fast and jerkily while her clothes refused to co-operate.

"It has." He helped her break free of the bra then moved her into a beam of slanting streetlight that had snuck into the room, and took the time to look at her topless and vulnerable, conveying with his eyes how much he liked what he saw.

Her nerves were quickly overcome by her desire, and after an eager glance at him she definitely liked what she saw, too. A combination of jitters and excitement flitted along her skin. He clamped his mouth on a breast, kissing and sucking, while he pushed on the waist of her pants.

On board with the total program, Polly understood this would be no-frills sex but long-overdue passion that could only be released in a flash and never fast enough. Ready for anything, everything, she squirmed out of her tight jeans and underpants while trying not to lose contact with his body.

Soon back to having her pressed to the wall, he sealed his lips tightly to hers and his heavy erection pressed into her belly. The rush and aroma of hot skin and stimulation made her squirm with need. His hand slid between her legs, fingers quickly discovering how ready she was. He positioned himself and she lifted her thigh and wrapped her calf around his waist so he could find her entrance.

Angling his full erection, he hesitated. "I don't have a condom."

"I'm on the Pill."

Her answer seemed to satisfy him, and he launched

into her, releasing a sizzling sensation that spread across her hips. A few more thrusts and she'd molded to his length and thickness, her moisture slickening him more with each move. The internal burning turned to smoldering and soon fire as he pushed into her over and over, setting off bells, whistles and alarms on every surface he touched.

It had been over a year since she'd made love with anyone, and her tightness intensified the sensations rolling through her pelvis and soon connecting with the shivers in her breasts. She ached for more as he drove into her again and again, thrilling her, making her beg he'd never stop.

Under the hold of his strong arms, her body banged against the wall. He emitted deep, throaty sounds as he continued to bury himself inside her hard and fast, seeming desperate to have all of her. As if humanly possible, he grew harder with each thrust. Though wanting to ride with him all the way to his climax, she couldn't hold out. Her mounting thrill became too intense to control as crazy sensations spilled out and over her like demons storming through her body. She gasped and bit his shoulder as she came, helpless to stop the powerful release. His continued forceful rhythm extended her climax until she was as limp as a ragdoll against him.

With an "Ahh" he came and she felt his warmth spread inside. With spasm after spasm she adjusted her hips and drew him even deeper than he'd been as he crumpled against her. They stayed in that position, she limp, he holding her flush to the wall, locked tightly together until every last tingle and pulse from the top of her head to the tips of her breasts and all the way down to the soles of her feet completed their course.

Taking her chin in the V of his hand, he bussed her

lightly on the lips. Near feral eyes burned into hers when he drew back. "I'm not through with you yet," he whispered.

Too numb to speak, she stared at him mesmerized, completely willing to be with him again, however he wanted it.

Still bound together, he carried her just as they were against the wall towards the small bed, as if she were a feather. With her legs still wrapped securely around his hips, he slowly and gently placed her beneath him on the mattress, careful not to lose their point of contact. Amazingly, he was still firm.

With a serious-as-hell gaze he lifted her arms above her head and clamped one hand tightly around her wrists, binding her to the bed. He bent and took a breast into his mouth and cupped the other with his free hand. Minutes passed with his soft, sexy torture of kisses here and nips there, his intensifying touch drawing her nearer and nearer to frenzy. When she squirmed and tried to free her hands he held her firm, completely in charge. Already on overdrive, every touch, nibble and kiss sent her reeling. She wanted more and more.

After a few more minutes he grew harder inside her and slowly began to move in and out, each thrust building force. Still a prisoner to his hold, she moved the only part she could, her hips. She matched his pace, adjusting her position to bring him closer, being rewarded with amazing sensations gathering and tightening in her core. Within a few more minutes he was back to full strength, and as he drove faster and deeper, her thrills intensified, coiling so tight she neared another release.

As if he could feel her mounting climax around him, still clamping her hands over her head, he broke contact with her breast, accelerated his thrusts, and smiled devilishly at her. "There's definitely an advantage to having sex with a people-pleaser," he said, quickly finishing her off.

Embarrassed by how easy she'd been to conquer, again, she laughed while she came, a complete first for her. He let go of her wrists and rolled onto his back, bringing her along. She straddled his waist and held tight, soon taking him right where she wanted him, helpless to resist her and completely at her mercy, just as she'd been with him only moments before.

After he'd come, she smiled down at him, kissed and licked the crease of his curled lips. "I'm not through with you yet," she said.

It was his turn to laugh. "So I *have* died and gone to heaven, huh?"

She rubbed her breasts across his chest and nestled into the crook of his neck, taking his earlobe between her teeth. "I haven't even known you for a week, Johnny," she whispered into his ear.

His hands cupped her bottom and squeezed tight, sparking new desire. "Crazy, isn't it?"

"Crazy good?"

"Definitely."

Before dawn, Polly woke up tangled up in John's arms and legs. The word "crazy" occurred to her again as she disengaged, used the shower, dressed and snuck out before John woke up. As it was her weekend off, she couldn't be seen sneaking out of the on-call room by any of her co-workers arriving on Saturday morning for the day shift without stirring questions. Fully dressed, hair damp and on her shoulders, she tiptoed outside, but not before glancing over her shoulder at John, who slept peacefully, then she quietly latched the door.

Lying there, listening to Polly shower and dress, John played possum when she left. Truth was he didn't know what to say to her. They'd amazed each other with great sex half the night, finally collapsing from exhaustion in each other's arms only a few short hours ago. He'd never let go so soon or so easily with anyone in his life until Polly the people-pleaser had arrived on his doorstep.

He scrubbed his face to help him wake up. What the hell should he do now? It was so out of character for him to screw an employee. The thought of running into her on the ward would be awkward as hell after everything they'd done to each other. How could he keep professional with her now?

He wasn't looking for a relationship. She was too damn young for him. Too sweet for her own good. Too wild and crazy in bed for a man still pining for his wife. He would be just as bad for her as that jerk she'd come to talk to him about. Why did the thought of Polly being with another man make his blood boil again, especially now that he'd made love to her? What right did he have to feel possessive of her? Wasn't he as bad as that guy after the way he'd brought her here to the on-call room for the sole purpose of making love until the burning she caused inside him finally stopped?

Thinking about her this morning, he realized the desire for her hadn't come close to burning out. But it had to. John Griffin didn't have gratuitous sex, especially with someone vulnerable like Polly. Or someone he worked with. He sat at the side of the bed, ran his fingers through his hair as he stood and headed for the shower. What about Lisa?

There were too many questions, but only one answer seemed to solve them all. He'd avoid Polly as much as possible, and once he worked out in his head just what the hell had happened last night and why, he'd explain to her that it was unethical and could never happen again. She'd have to understand.

That was his plan, and he'd have to stick to it, because he wasn't about to change his just-getting-by personal life for a flighty young thing like Polly Seymour.

Polly got on the subway heading for the Lower East Side. Not knowing what to say to him, she hadn't been able to get away from John fast enough. What had gotten into her? Granted, he'd taken her to the on-call room after giving her the most incredible foot massage of her life and, well, they'd taken the natural course from there. And wow. She hadn't held back, and neither had he. Never in her life had she done such a thing, had sex with a man she hardly knew. A man she worked for!

Sitting on the hard seat of the subway train, she wondered if everyone in the car, which was thankfully only a handful, could see her flush until her ears burned. She rested her head against the cold window and stared out at the quickly passing darkness. She wasn't about to act needy around Johnny Griffin. No. That would turn him off quicker than her kisses had turned him on. She'd have to ride out this awkward situation, see where John took it. As far as she was concerned, it was up to him to approach her. After the way she'd made love with him, the man at least owed her a thank you.

Allowing her mind to drift back to the night before and some of the amazing things that had occurred, she remembered that "thank you" swung both ways. Holy cow, did it ever.

On Monday morning Polly arrived at work with trepidation. Her palms tingled and her stomach clenched at the thought of facing the head of Orthopedics. Doubt upon doubt had cropped up over the weekend. Was having sex in the on-call room how Dr. Griffin initiated all the new nurses?

In her heart she knew that wasn't true. He loathed interacting with his staff, and after a week on the job she hadn't heard any rumors about his personal life... just that he was a loner who preferred the kids on the ortho ward to adult company.

Surprised to see that Annabelle had already been discharged, she took report on all new patients. Today she'd be nurse to four pre-teens in various sizes and shaped casts in a group ward.

In the middle of taking vital signs she heard John's voice outside. Nerves unfurled through her center, making her hands shake. Still unprepared to face him, she prayed he'd stay out in the nurses' station area and not come into her room.

The deep, masculine tone carried over the usual noise of the ward as he spoke to Brooke. "Tell your nurses to get their kids ready by nine."

Polly was still getting used to the non-stop activities of Angel's Children's Hospital. They even had an on-site radio show in the lobby, and often the kids were the subjects of interviews. The play therapists didn't allow the patients to zone out on video games or too much TV. They kept them interacting with other patients with games and challenges where everyone could participate. If a child was too sick to leave their room, they'd come to them.

Volunteer grandmothers and grandfatherly types regularly came for one-to-one bedside reading, and the children ate it up. Especially with the man who looked like Santa on his day off in a Hawaiian shirt and golf cap reading *Harry Potter* cover to cover.

Polly snuck a look outside her room just in time to see John turn and walk back toward his office on the far side of the hospital wing. Though not a tall man, his broad shoulders reminded her how strong he was. A quick flash of him naked and carrying her to the bed in the on-call room had her cheeks burning.

"Why're you red?" the girl with waist-length black hair and a full leg cast asked. "Do you have a fever or something?"

"No. I'm fine. Don't you ever blush?"

"Not unless I'm embarrassed. Are you embarrassed?" Her insightful, inquisitive eyes made Polly's skin crawl.

"Maybe a little."

"Why?"

Polly glanced around the brightly decorated four-bed ward, where stenciled sports equipment and swaths of primary colors made the white walls pop, as she searched for either a dodge or a believable answer. One thing she'd quickly learned working with kids was they could tell when someone wasn't being straight with them.

"I just remembered something I did over the weekend."

"Did you get hammered?" The young one's bright black eyes suddenly seemed far too mature for twelve.

"No. And how do you even know what 'hammered' means?"

"My sister goes to college." She tossed half of her hair over her shoulder, in a gesture that advertised she knew everything about being a grown up and drinking too much in college.

As if that explained and closed the topic, Polly let the subject drop, but not before she noticed John Griffin's signature on the girl's cast and she felt her cheeks flush again. Did the man sign every single cast on the ward?

As promised, at nine o'clock sharp a raucous brass quartet blustered onto the ward playing circus music, as if a parade would follow. Polly had gotten each of her patients into wheelchairs and rolled them to the center of the ward just in time. One of her girls wasn't the least bit interested in the music, instead staring at her cell phone, until the trombone player swung by and hit a low note by extending the slide right under her chin. It shocked and delighted her and Polly laughed along with the patient, especially when the girl glanced up and saw a good-looking college guy, and her eyes brightened.

In mid-laugh, Polly glanced up and caught John's gaze from across the room. It seemed a trapdoor had opened in her chest, and her heart skidded to her ankles. Maybe it was the circus music.

She couldn't inhale.

Attempting and falling far short of the mark, she gave some semblance of a smile, and in return he gave that half grimace, half smile he was so adept at then quickly looked away.

Could things get any more awkward?

By Wednesday afternoon, having great sex with John Griffin had started to seem more like a figment of Polly's imagination than fact. He'd drifted in and out of the hospital ward like a ghost leaving hints of things out of place, or the tell-tale scent of his woodsy aftershave, or an icy chill spiraling down her spine. Not once did he try to confront her, and she'd vowed to steer clear of his office no matter how much she wanted to chew him out for being so cold and inconsiderate for leaving her dangling and insecure since Friday night.

On Thursday morning the pet therapy Dalmatian made rounds, stopping beside Polly's toddler patient, Eugenia. The child had fallen from a two-story window and broken both arms, and had been taken into protective services after being admitted to Angel's. She was withdrawn and moody, and Polly didn't know how to reach her or make her comfortable. But Dotty the Dalmatian brightened the child's gray eyes with interest, and soon a smile crossed her lips as Dotty licked her fingertips.

Warmth washed through Polly's down mood, and she grinned at her young charge, then was rewarded with Eugenia smiling back. Simple things. Small steps. This was the way to put a life back together, as Polly only knew too well from her own childhood.

"May I talk to you?" From behind, the familiar voice made her eyes go wide. It was John. Adrenaline sprayed like scattershot throughout her chest. She schooled her expression before she turned.

"Sure," she said, acting as if nothing, especially her ego, had been flipped sideways since they'd had mind-blowing sex.

Leaving her patient with Dotty and the pet therapy lady, she followed his long and purposeful strides toward the supply room.

When they arrived, he took a deep breath. "I don't want this to be offensive or anything," he said in a nearly inaudible voice, "but I think you should take some STD tests."

So this was all about medical business, about the messy little clean-up committee for being reckless with the new girl. He may not have wanted to offend her but pure insult made her send him a cutting glance. "Why, Doctor? Have you jeopardized me?"

"No!" he rasped. She could see the vein on the side of his neck pop out.

"But you worry I may have…"

"No," he said, in a strained whisper. "I'm just being practical."

She latched onto his eyes and stared him down. "For your information, I don't sleep around. I don't have any surprises to give you, so I'll skip. Thanks." She turned to walk away, trying her best to save what was left of her pride, but he caught her by the elbow and held her back.

"We were completely careless." He spoke quietly, directly into her ear. Even now, under the worst possible circumstances, the touch of his breath on her neck made her skin prickle. She looked up at him. His dark eyes peered into hers in warning. "As a doctor, I can't be negligent. I've ordered some tests for you."

"What about you?" she said, hackles fully raised and ready to fight.

He looked thoughtfully at his OR clogs. "I checked out okay."

"Then what's the point of me—?"

His flat expression warned she wasn't about to like his answer. "Because I'm not the one who can get pregnant, even if you're on birth control pills."

Stunned by reality, she swallowed around a dry knot. She'd already told him there wouldn't be a problem— didn't he believe her? Since he was being such a jerk about everything today, she wouldn't argue.

Desperate to save face, she shrugged free of his hold. "I'll handle the tests myself, thanks," she said as she walked away, trying her best to stand straight and look confident, while feeling anything but.

That night, still fuming, she stopped at the corner ma and pa grocery store and found a pregnancy test purporting to identify a pregnancy within seven to ten days after the missed period. But Polly hadn't missed her period, which wasn't due for another three days. Would she be able to hold tight and wait for three days then buy the test? The blood test John had ordered could tell much sooner than the urine test, but her pride had tripped her up and kept her from consenting. She was sure that just because John Griffin had ordered the test and the results would be sent to him, he wasn't going to be the first to know if, and that was a very big if, she was pregnant or not.

Of course she wasn't pregnant. She took her pills every night as directed.

For some illogical reason, that night when she prepared her dinner she made sure it was well balanced and nutritious as one short phrase whispered in her mind—*What if?*—which was quickly followed by a heavy brick of panic landing in her stomach and replacing her appetite.

Monday morning, officially late for her period, Polly showed up at work withdrawn and anxious. Dread trickled down her spine as she remembered the antibiotics she'd taken a few weeks back for a sinus infection. It was a known fact that antibiotics could interfere with the potency of birth control pills for up to two weeks. It had been more than two weeks since she'd taken them, though, and that kept her hopeful all would be fine.

"Hey, Polly, how's it shakin'?" the ward clerk Rafael asked as she passed the nurses' station.

"Meh," she said, and walked on.

"What? If you're not in a good mood, how the heck am I supposed to be?"

She stopped in her tracks and saw honest surprise in his dark chocolate-colored eyes. "I guess you'll just have to work extra hard at it today, Rafe ol' buddy."

"That's cold, forcing a man to be in a good mood for no good reason all on his own." He laughed. "See, even in a bad mood you make me smile."

"What's this I hear about little Miss Sunshine being in a foul mood?" Brooke said, approaching Polly and putting her hand on Polly's shoulder. She rubbed back and forth. "You okay?"

Did her face have to be an open book?

"I've been better." She should have gotten her period on Saturday, but so far there wasn't even a hint that it was on the way. She had a question she wanted to ask Brooke, but didn't want to be blatant about how a person went about getting a pregnancy test done at Angel's, so she decided to wait for a better time under less obvious circumstances.

On Wednesday morning, Brooke assigned her once again to Eugenia, who was constantly being assessed and visited by social services, play therapists, speech therapists, and just about every doctor on staff. Polly looked forward to spending the day with a little girl who needed love as much as she did.

During Eugenia's bed bath, Polly tickled and teased the child to get her to laugh, which she did more easily this week than last.

"Mornin', peanut," a woman with a heavy Texan drawl said. "How's my girl today?"

Polly looked up to see the beautiful blonde Dr. Layla Woods. "Can you say good morning for Dr. Woods, Eugenia?"

"Mun."

Dr. Woods smiled at Polly, then at Eugenia. "That's very good."

Polly loved her accent. As Dr. Woods warmed the child up with a game of peek-a-boo and then delicately did a quick physical assessment of Eugenia, Polly studied her flawless complexion and gorgeous Texas-bluebell-colored eyes. She'd seen her before on the orthopedic floor several times making general medicine rounds, always smiling and gracious. Always approachable.

Polly had heard rumblings about Dr. Woods and the head of Neurosurgery, Dr. Alejandro Rodriguez, the most gorgeous man on the planet. Bar none. But she didn't want to get caught up in hospital gossip and had paid little attention to the stories.

She looked back at the doctor, who'd finished up her examination of Eugenia with a tap on the tip of the toddler's nose. Dr. Woods could easily be a cover model or actress with her good looks, but there was an added ingredient, sort of like a secret sauce, that made the whole recipe of Layla Woods extra-special. Perhaps seasoned by her own life, the woman oozed compassion.

And that's when it hit her. No risk, no gain, right?

Polly cleared her throat and worked up the fortitude to ask the question of the day. "Dr. Woods, um, may I ask you a favor?"

"Sure, whatcha' need?"

"Could you order me a pregnancy test?" she mumbled, embarrassed.

"A pregnancy test?"

Polly wanted to shush her, but didn't have the nerve, instead lowering her lashes and staring at the floor. The perceptive doctor quickly caught on.

"Oh," she whispered, looking around. Thankfully no one else but the toddlers were in the two bed-ward. "Sorry. Certainly. I'll order that right now. You want a blood test, right?"

Polly nodded. "Thanks so much."

Dr. Woods winked, jotting down Polly's last name from her name badge, then Polly gave her medical record number.

"Your secret's safe with me. Good luck, whichever way you hope it turns out." She smiled and after pinching Eugenia's cheeks and kissing her forehead the lovely doctor left the room, heading for the nearby computer to input that order.

At the end of her shift Polly stopped at the lab to have her blood drawn. After a long day and a crowded subway ride home she was hot and exhausted and didn't look forward to taking those five flights of stairs up to her room. A room that didn't even have air-conditioning. If this was how it got in early July, how would she survive the rest of the summer?

While making a mental note to buy a big fan, she let herself into the apartment. Mrs. Goldman, her landlady, sat in the tiny, dim living room watching TV and didn't even look up, which Polly was glad about. The last thing she wanted to do was get sucked into one of her landlady's long and meandering stories tonight. After a snack she slipped into her room and took a nap.

A couple of hours later she decided to check her e-mails and saw the notice from Angel's hospital about her test results. Quickly accessing the hospital patient medical records program, she went into her account, eager to end this chapter in her book of life's mistakes. The sooner she knew all was clear, the faster she could close the door for good on John Griffin and move on.

She'd sweep her regretful actions into a corner and forget about them, like she had so many other things in her life. Though forgetting her incredible night with John would take a lot of effort.

Opening up her lab test page, her hopeful attitude got hitched to gravity and plummeted into an abyss. Positive. The blood test was positive.

Prickles of fear stormed like a battalion across her skin as her entire body went hot.

She. Was. Pregnant.

CHAPTER FIVE

FRIDAY MORNING, JOHN sat at his desk on the computer finishing up the last of his administrative work, the thing he liked least about being a department head. If he had his way he'd do surgery every day, but he needed to play fair and share the admin duties with his orthopedic surgical staff.

Out of habit, he glanced at the spot on his desk he'd always looked when in doubt, but it was empty. He'd already forgotten that he'd put the framed photograph of his wife in the desk drawer the previous week. He hadn't been able to look at her picture without feeling guilty since he'd slept with Polly...even though it had been twelve years since Lisa had died.

He wasn't a saint, he'd been with a woman here or there over the years, but never had he gotten involved, and he liked it that way. That was, until Polly and this alien desire to get involved. Very involved.

He thought about her every day, relived their love-making in his head at the craziest moments, and even though he'd handled everything monumentally badly, he still smiled when he thought about her lively blue eyes, sexy grin, and perky young body.

Polly the people-pleaser extraordinaire.

At thirty-nine he was too young for a midlife crisis,

wasn't he? With his elbow on the desk, he sank his chin into the palm of his hand and looked out the window. Damn, he'd become a moony teenager all over again.

Couldn't he just apologize to her for being so crass and start over?

Truth was he wanted to, and he'd never thought of himself as a coward…

The tap at the door yanked him from his thoughts. "Come in."

When Polly stepped into the room, looking tired and worried, something thick and cold dropped in his stomach and she got his full attention. Barely able to lift her eyes to his, she walked toward his desk.

He shot up from his chair. "Are you all right?"

She sighed and sat, finally lifting her gaze to meet his. "Yes, actually, I am."

He sat, not wanting to be a pushover. "Can you forgive me for being a jerk?" His mouth had gotten a jump on his cool-and-calm plan.

"That depends."

"On?"

"On how you react when I tell you something."

Another sinking feeling slithered down John's throat. What messy surprise was she going to spring on him? Would she tell him she never wanted to be with him again when he'd just realized how much he wanted to know her better? He sat perfectly still, keeping her in his line of vision, waiting for her big announcement. To cover his insecurity, he went the tough route.

"I'm a big boy. Don't worry about me." He thought about picking up his pen and pretending to continue to work on his papers, blowing her off, just to show her how absolutely fine he was with however she planned to dump him. Yes, he was a busy, busy man, who would hardly notice if she dropped out of his life.

Liar.

She put her fingertips over her mouth and watched him, as if gauging his true feelings. Shaking her head, she glanced at the floor then back up at him. "There's no easy way to put this."

He went still, sensing the heaviness in the room gather into a giant cloud directly over his head. This wasn't the Polly he knew. This Polly seemed like she'd been steamrollered by life, not the bright young woman she'd been when she'd first arrived at Angel's...before they'd made love.

Pretty lousy effect you have on women, Griffin.

Okay, he'd made a snap decision. He wouldn't mess up her life one more day, no matter how badly he wanted to get involved. She didn't deserve a moody old fart like him.

"I'm pregnant."

He'd let her go, break it off clean— What?

"You're pregnant?" He'd checked his lab reports every day and hadn't seen her results. "And you know this how?"

"I asked Dr. Woods to order a blood test for me." She raised her hand. "Before you say another word I want to tell you straight out that I will not end this pregnancy. And I don't intend to give up the baby for adoption." She looked into his eyes, hers shining from moisture. "I know how it feels not to be wanted..." her voice broke with emotion "...and I won't let my baby go through that." She swallowed and sat quietly, obviously trying to hold herself together.

He'd heard everything she'd said. He'd paid attention.

Yet he needed to repeat the words, to make them real, and help them sink in. "You're pregnant."

"Yes."

With his hands on his desk, perfectly still, he leaned forward, trying to get his mouth to move so he could ask the question *What do we do now?* but nothing came out.

"And no matter what you say…" she stared at him out of those determined, teary eyes, having the same effect as reaching into his chest and wrenching out his heart "…I'm keeping this baby."

His baby. She was keeping his baby. He'd never thought he'd have a chance at a family again. A nugget of hope planted itself in his heart, filling a long-forgotten hole. He almost smiled at the absurdity of how he'd become a father at thirty-nine—from one amazing night in on-call.

Not since his wife had told him she was pregnant had he felt such a flash of joy.

A baby. A family.

But that had been long ago, and six weeks before 9/11. When he'd loved and lost both his wife and unborn child. When he would have gladly given his own life in exchange for theirs.

A jet of fear shot through his chest and strangled the breath out of him. He couldn't speak as a flashback of the hopeless feeling that had nearly ended his life—and had surely ended his wife and future child's life—played out in his head. The horror of that day. The frantic need to find her in the rubble. The sinking feeling as reality had put one foot in front of the other and stepped ever closer to ripping his life apart, as it had for so many others. The desperation when hope against all the odds had lost out and he'd found out she'd been killed. That he'd never kiss Lisa again, never hold her, never welcome their baby into his arms.

Oh, God, he couldn't do this again. He couldn't bear the pain if anything happened to this baby...or Polly. He'd used up an entire life's worth of pain and sadness already. He couldn't spare one more...

"Are you all right?"

Polly's gentle voice broke through his thoughts. Even when confessing her predicament, she'd put him first. Was he all right? What about *her*? Was *she* all right with him getting her pregnant? Of course not! Yet, trouper that she was, she'd come to tell him she was keeping their baby, whether he liked it or not.

He tried to unclench his fists, to act as if he hadn't just relived the worst day of his life. Unfortunately, his expression must have been a snapshot of his true feelings, and Polly was a solid people-reader. Perspiration moistened his upper lip. He rubbed it away.

"Yes, I'm all right." He took a deep breath, knowing it would be impossible to invest emotionally in this pregnancy. At least he could be a civilized man and offer financial support. Surely she couldn't do this on her own without his monetary help. He ground his molars and lifted his eyes to meet her steady and earnest gaze. "How much do you think you'll need?"

His hands shook so badly he wasn't even sure he'd be able to hold a pen if she agreed to let him write her a check. He held onto the desk rim to hide his shaking.

He may as well have slapped her face by the way she flinched at his words. "Pardon?" Anger, like an off-shore squall, gathered in those luminescent blue eyes. Her face tensed, incensed. "You think I came here to ask for money?" Her voice quivered with barely controlled rage. "You want to pay me because you knocked me up?"

Of course she'd take it the wrong way. She didn't have a clue what he'd been through, and he sure as hell didn't have the strength to tell her now. He had to hold it together, to be the worst kind of bastard on earth in order to make it through this meeting. No matter what she thought of him, she at least deserved to be well taken care of.

He tugged his earlobe. "That's right." His jaw was so tightly locked the words had to squeeze themselves out.

Her obviously escalating fury forced her to stand. Her cheeks blushed red, her eyes looked wild. "You bastard!"

It was her turn to verbally slap *him*. "This pregnancy isn't some little problem you can clean up with cash. For me it's sacred!" She stormed out of the room and slammed the door, leaving the glass and walls shaking as much as his hands.

Ah, hell. He picked up his pen and tossed it across the desk. Could he have handled the situation any worse?

Almost a week later Polly helped her favorite LVN, Darren, start an IV he'd accidentally dislodged. She sat at the hospital bedside with her IV kit prepared and in reach. Children were always a challenge, and the little boy had started screaming the moment he'd realized what the "lady nurse" was going to do to him. Darren firmly held the six-year-old's arm to the bed, his other arm safely secured in a cast and sling. With Darren's free hand he pressed against the boy's knees to control the fidgeting legs.

Starting an IV on a child that was freaking out was

bad enough, but hitting a moving target was nearly impossible.

She wiped the skin with disinfectant and slipped on gloves. His wails escalated.

"Mikey, if you hold still for just a couple of seconds, this will go a lot quicker," Darren said. "Then I'll play *Battle Star* with you, I promise."

Fortunately, that morning the high school of performing arts had sent a troupe of street performers to their ward. A lanky kid in a fluorescent green shirt and a bright red beret appeared at the doorway, juggling neon yellow and blue bowling pins. He edged to the side of the bed, capturing the boy's attention.

The moment the child became distracted Polly slid the needle into the vein and anchored it with tape before Mikey's delayed protest made him squirm again. His mouth gaped as the juggler pretended, in an exaggerated way, to almost drop a pin.

"It's all over," Polly said. "Just need to tape it, Mikey." She wasn't even sure he was listening. "Then you can kick Darren's patootie in *Battle Star*, okay?"

The relieved child looked at his arm to make sure Polly hadn't lied, just as the juggler migrated to the next room.

Darren glanced at Polly, winked and smiled. She smiled back, then patted Mikey's shoulder. Teamwork. It was the only way to survive in a hospital.

Teamwork in a pregnancy was pretty darned important, too.

Leaving the room, she almost ran into John, who was holding a tiny patient and watching the juggler as he switched to multicolored balls. It had been a week since she'd told him she was pregnant and had stormed out of his office after he'd insulted her, and he hadn't lifted a finger to contact her since. She yanked herself back before they made physical contact, as her heart nearly hurtled out of her chest. "Oh, sorry," she said, by rote.

He handed the tiny patient to the nearby nurse then steadied Polly by holding her arms. "My fault. Wasn't watching where I was going."

She stared at his feet, rather than look at him, furious with him, the feel of his warm hands on her skin almost her undoing. What could she say that she hadn't already confessed in his office, and he'd frozen her out, tried to pay her off, leaving her hurt beyond comprehension? She'd calmed down since then for her baby's sake, and from now on her baby would be the only thing she cared about.

She stepped back, removing her arms from his grasp. The last thing she needed was for anyone on staff to become suspicious about them, or find out about their predicament. *Her* predicament, as he'd have nothing to do with it. The pregnancy would be apparent to everyone soon enough.

"How are you feeling?" he asked, under his breath.

"Fine. Thank you." She walked away, pretending her legs didn't feel like noodles, holding her head high. She felt his eyes on her, but refused to turn round.

"Dr. Griffin! Dr. Griffin!" a child's voice cried out. "Will you make me an elephant?"

"I'll make you two elephants, if you'll quit giving your physical therapist such a hard time, Nate."

Did he even give a damn about her?

The boy laughed, and Polly could practically see John messing his hair and pretending to punch him in the arm with the cast. The man was a natural with kids, yet he'd chosen to ignore his own child.

* * *

Later that day, when the opportunity came up to work a double shift, Polly jumped at the chance. She'd need to work lots of double shifts to earn as much money as possible while she could for her and the baby.

The evening staff had a whole different feel from the day crew. Gossip seemed to be their favorite pastime, and Polly got an earful from another RN named Janetta, a large woman with a loud voice. When Janetta spoke, everyone listened.

"You know that pretty new blonde doctor, Layla something or other?" Janetta said.

"Dr. Woods?" Polly asked.

"Mmm-hmm. That's the one. She talks weird."

"She's from Texas."

"That's right, honey. That's the one." Janetta leaned forward and looked around. "Guess who she's having an affair with."

Polly didn't have a clue, neither did she want to know, but something told her Janetta was about to tell her anyway.

"Dr. Dreamy himself. That hunk from Neuro, Dr. Rodriguez."

Come to think of it, Layla and Dr. Rodriguez would make a perfect couple, but Polly kept her thoughts to herself. "How do you know they're having an affair?"

"Everyone knows it. Where have you been? It's the talk of the hospital. Goes way back. I heard from a good source that it broke up Dr. Woods's marriage, too. It must be true, 'cos she's single."

The thought of her own and John's personal business getting spread all over the hospital like poor Dr. Woods and Dr. Rodriguez made her skin prickle.

From the corner of her eye she noticed John entering room number one. "Goodnight, Chloe and Sandra. Sleep tight. See you in the morning light."

She'd never been here before for John's nightly ritual.

He zipped into the next room. "Jason and Brandon, don't give your nurses a hard time or you'll have to answer to me. Have a good night's sleep and I'll be back to check on you tomorrow."

How would John hold his head up at work if their affair became fodder for the hospital gossip mill?

As for herself, she couldn't wait to be a mother, single or not. Finally she'd have a baby to love and cherish and they'd be a family, just the two of them. She thought about Dr. Woods and wondered if she had a clue what was being said about her, and decided not to participate in this grapevine.

She thought about telling Janetta that unless she knew for sure about something, she shouldn't pass it along, but didn't want to get on Janetta's bad side. Instead, she nodded her head and let Janetta give her the rundown on several other people having affairs in the hospital, while listening to John enter each patient room and wishing the children a good night.

Soon enough her name would be added to the jilted-lover list.

Polly kept her thoughts to herself and to avoid John went back to caring for her patients, thankful that visiting hours made the floor busier and noisier than usual. The chaos still wasn't enough to keep her from thinking about her own situation, though.

She'd have to get used to the evening staff as she planned to work at least two extra shifts a month from now until she went on maternity leave. She would have to in order to make ends meet, and there was no way she'd let John pay her for getting her pregnant. She'd never take his guilt money.

Thankfully, she'd get medical coverage through Angel's hospital after her probationary two months. She'd have to hold tight until then to have her first prenatal appointment. Since she didn't have a clue how to find a good obstetrician in town, she'd have to be discreet about getting a name without alerting the rest of the staff to her situation.

During her dinner break Janetta and someone Polly had never seen before joined her at the only table in the nurses' lounge.

"This here is Vickie. She's the receptionist up in hospital Administration offices."

Polly greeted her, but wondered what she was doing hanging around the hospital after hours. The look on Vickie's face made Polly think she was bursting with something to say.

"I thought we were going to be alone," Vickie said to Janetta.

"Oh, you can trust Polly. Now, spill. What's the big news you have for me?"

Vickie licked her lips as excitement widened her eyes. "You'll never believe what happened today."

"Go on, go on." Janetta practically rubbed her hands together with glee.

"Okay. Well, Dr. Woods got called up to the offices today. She showed up all solemn-faced and nervous. When they buzzed me and I told her to go inside, girl, she looked scared." Vickie took a big bite of bread and chewed quickly.

Janetta impatiently gobbled some of her dinner, as if not wanting to miss a single syllable. Polly wished she could disappear, but knew if she walked out Janetta would peg her as someone she couldn't trust with good old-fashioned gossip, which would make Polly an enemy, so she stayed in her chair, quietly nibbling at her meal.

Vickie's eyes brightened. "Okay, so a couple minutes after Dr. Woods is in the room, guess who comes barreling through the office doors?"

"Tell me, oh, tell me. Not…"

"Yes. Dr. R., and before the door can close I hear him say 'I insist Dr. Woods's name be cleared'."

"Cleared from what?" Janetta looked like she was sitting around a campfire hearing a famous urban legend being retold.

"I think this has to do with some surgery on a kid back in Los Angeles that they got sued for. But get this. I sort of got out of my chair and went over by the door so I could hear better. He says, 'She's a gifted doctor with much to offer our hospital, and she shouldn't have her name dragged through the media because of a surgery I agreed to perform'." Vickie put on a horrible accent, and Polly's stomach twisted with guilt, listening. "'I was the person who was charged in that malpractice suit, not Dr. Woods, and I was cleared.' He went on to say that he knew the surgery would be high risk, and if they wanted to lay the blame on anyone, it should be him."

"Oh, my God, this is something."

"Yeah, so next thing I know, Dr. Woods rushes out of the offices and out the door and Dr. Rodriguez keeps yelling at them. The last thing I heard was, *'No, you listen to me. The verdict was no malpractice. Make it public, then!'*"

Janetta was practically salivating over this news. Polly sat silent, watching the two women live vicariously through someone else's drama. It just didn't seem right.

Later, while exiting her patient's room, she noticed the nurses' station had gone quiet. She glanced up and spotted across the ward the very doctor Janetta and Vickie had been talking about at dinner. Polly waved and rushed to her side, not caring how it looked to her co-workers.

"Hi," Dr. Woods said with a genuine glad-to-see-you smile.

"Hi. I wanted to thank you for arranging my test, and ask another question if you don't mind?"

"Of course not. What's up?"

Polly guided Dr. Woods to a more private spot, noticing Janetta's eagle eyes watching. She lowered her voice. "I was wondering if you could recommend an obstetrician who is close by the hospital."

Layla raised a perfectly arched brow. "So the test was positive," she whispered.

Polly gave one solemn nod.

Layla patted her forearm. "Let me ask around, since I'm kind of new in town myself, and I'll get back to you, 'kay?"

"Thank you so much."

"Darlin', it's my pleasure. We girls gotta to stick together. You know?"

Overwhelmed by the doctor's care and genuine concern, once their hushed conversation had ended, Polly decided that regardless of the hospital gossip about Dr. Woods having had an affair with the head of Neurosurgery while she was still married, Polly would be Layla Woods's number one fan.

Polly could barely breathe when on the following Thursday the case involving Dr. Woods and Rodriguez went public at Angel's. She read the memo addressed to the hospital staff about a boy named Jamie Kilpatrick and a high-risk neurosurgery that Dr. Woods had recommended to Dr. Rodriguez. One thing stood out beyond everything else: Dr. Rodriguez had valiantly taken full responsibility for the boy's death.

One major question crossed Polly's mind. Why would Dr. Rodriguez put his career and reputation on the line to protect Dr. Woods? She didn't need to think for long. The man was obviously in love with her, just like Janetta had said. Wow, what must it feel like to have someone love you that much?

That night Polly combed the aisles of her local market, hunting for healthy food. Her routine in the mornings had always been to buy a couple of pieces of fresh fruit from one of the street carts near the hospital. She'd bring a yogurt from home for morning break, then a sandwich for lunch, usually tuna, and eat the second piece of fruit. Now she worried she wasn't getting enough vitamins. She grabbed a bag of baby spinach, deciding to sauté it with oil and garlic and serve it for dinner over the chicken breast she'd just picked up. Eating for two was a big responsibility, and she wanted her baby to have the best opportunity possible at a healthy start.

Eyeing a package of her favorite cookies, she steered away. This pregnancy business would be harder than anything she'd done in her life, but she was determined to have a successful pregnancy.

The thought of a healthy baby brought back the need to see an obstetrician in the next couple of weeks. With fingers crossed that Dr. Woods would come through for her, she paid for her groceries and headed home.

* * *

John stood over his six-burner state-of-the-art stove, grilling salmon. He'd gutted the old-fashioned kitchen when his parents had sold him their condo at a steal before moving to Florida. Now he had a kitchen that connected to the flow of the house, instead of hidden behind a wall. The 56th Street, near Sutton Place address was perfectly situated for work, plus he had the East River within walking distance whenever he felt like taking a jog. With two bedrooms and baths, a living room, which he'd expanded by breaking down a small third bedroom wall, and the new roomier kitchen, he lived comfortably for a New York City bachelor.

Tri-colored squash sautéed in a small pan and the brown rice steamed in another. He loved to cook and wasn't shy about letting people know. While cooking, he wondered if Polly was taking good care of herself, and how she might enjoy this meal. Flipping the fish, he realized he didn't have a clue what she liked to eat beyond cheese pizza. For all he knew, she hated fish.

She was carrying his baby. Every time he thought about it, the breath squeezed from his lungs.

With everything under control dinner-wise, and Polly solidly implanted in his mind, he dug out his cell phone and called a forgotten friend. "Geoff, it's John."

The old medical school colleagues went through a required, though brief catch-up time, then John broached the true reason for his call. "I was wondering if you'd do me a favor. One of my ortho nurses just found out she's pregnant, and she needs a good OB guy. I told her I knew the best. Any chance you could squeeze her in?"

Geoff asked John to hold while he flipped through his calendar and, taking this opportunity, John checked the salmon and veggies, then opened his kitchen catch-all drawer, hunting for a pad of paper and a pen. Soon Geoff was back on the line with an appointment date and time.

"Fantastic. Thanks so much." He tugged his earlobe. "Oh, by the way, send me the bill."

By the brief silence on the other end before Geoff agreed, John figured he hadn't pulled the wool over his old classmate's eyes. Yes. John Griffin had knocked up a nurse. His nurse. Polly.

On Friday afternoon Polly was in the middle of hanging intravenous antibiotics for her newest post-op patient when John appeared at her side. Her hand trembled as she placed the small bottle of potent medicine on the hook and opened the drip regulator. She got mad at herself for letting him have that much power over her and hoped he hadn't noticed. He was in his OR scrubs, having followed the surgical patient back to the ward.

Having already received report from the OR recovery nurse, she knew Emanuel had been in a car accident, had broken his left leg, and needed to have a metal plate and pins to secure his bones back in place.

"I wanted you to have this." John handed her a small piece of paper.

She stared at it instead of reaching for it, thankful that Emanuel was completely out of it and in a private room so no one else would hear them talk. "What's that?"

"It's an appointment with the best OB guy in the city."

Hesitant to take anything from John, she shook her head. "That's okay. I've got someone else in mind."

John tugged his ear. "You need to let me be involved in this, too."

"Why, John? The other day you wanted nothing to do with me or our baby," she whispered spiritedly over Emanuel. "You wanted to pay me off." She wanted to sound indignant, but it came out hurt.

"Look, there's a lot to get used to for both of us. I'm just asking you to give me time."

She snatched the paper from his fingers. "You think I don't understand how much we both have to get used to? And as for time, well, you've got approximately eight months to work it out." She glanced at the appointment, next Thursday at four p.m. with a Geoffrey Bernstein. It was perfect for her work schedule, she'd give him that. Then she noticed the address. Park Avenue? "Forget it. I can't afford this guy."

"It's all taken care of."

It stalled her for a second, but she quickly recovered. "I don't want your guilt charity." She handed back the paper but he refused to take it and left, grinding his jaws, without another word.

That afternoon Layla Woods crossed the ward, heading directly for Polly, looking far less confident than usual. Up close, Polly could see she had dark circles under her eyes, as if she'd been on call and hadn't slept. "I've got some information for you."

"Great. Thank you so much." Polly glanced around to make sure no one was within hearing distance.

"I've been told this guy is the best OB doc in town. The only problem is the wait list is long, and I think he's pretty pricey." She handed Polly the paper, and Polly opened it immediately. *Dr. Geoffrey Bernstein.*

Polly tried not to hide her disappointment because Dr. Woods had gone out of her way to help her out. "I can't thank you enough. I'll look into this right away."

They parted company and Polly watched the petite

doctor walk away as a hollow, aching path burrowed through her stomach.

Round one had gone to John. Not only had he found her the most expensive doctor in town, he'd made an appointment for her, too. And he was paying.

As her least favorite Uncle Randolph used to say whenever Polly had resisted her cousin's baggy hand-me-down clothes: *Don't look a gift horse in the mouth.*

So be it. For the good of her baby she'd take the appointment John had made for her, and because she'd been raised right afterwards she'd swallow her pride and thank him for it.

Three nights later Polly worked her second double shift. It probably wasn't a wise move as she still hadn't recovered from the first sixteen-hour shift, even though she'd had the whole weekend to do it. Now she dragged through another.

The pregnancy had zapped most of her energy. She'd also become aware that other early signs of pregnancy were cropping up. Her breasts were tender, and she wanted to sleep more. And she was hungry. All the time. Maybe she'd be one of those lucky ladies who didn't get morning sickness, but it was still very early along.

For her dinner break, to avoid another gossip-infused lecture from Janetta, she decided to go outside and eat on a bench in the hospital garden. She walked to the elevator feeling more than fatigued, eager to breathe in some fresh air. With all of the gossip at the hospital and speculation about her own situation, she felt as though she had a brick on each shoulder. While she waited for the elevator she rolled her neck around and lifted her shoulders, hoping to release some stress from the stiff muscles.

The elevator pinged and opened to reveal Dr. Alex Rodriguez inside. Alone.

Polly had never seen the man up close before. She entered and tried not to stare at his handsome profile or notice the waves in his thick black hair as it curled along the collar of his shirt.

He stood stoically silent, deep in thought, hardly noticing she was there.

The elevator stopped at the next floor and Dr. Woods got on. Polly's heart tripled in beats. Layla nodded at Polly, looking noticeably riled, then turned to Dr. Rodriguez. "Hi," she said, sounding breathy and unconfident as she pressed the button for the lobby, which had already been pushed.

"Layla." His all-business attitude threw Polly in light of what she already knew about the memo and their supposed past, through Janetta.

"Listen, I wanted to thank you for what you did the other day," Layla said. "Sticking up for me in the board room and all."

"It needed to be done." Curt. Businesslike.

Had *she* become invisible?

"Well, I want to thank you for that, Alex. It meant a lot to—"

With a quick gesture, he brushed her off. "It was nothing." He wouldn't look her in the eyes, and that must have bothered Dr. Woods. It sure would have if Polly had been in the doctor's shoes.

Layla punched the button for the second floor, obviously upset. "Both of us getting out of the elevator together in the lobby would only fuel the fire of the gossip around here." She tossed her hair over her shoulder and the moment the doors opened she started to get out, but Dr. Rodriguez stepped around her and exited first.

Holy cow. Polly hoped and prayed that Layla didn't think she had participated in the rampant gossip around the hospital. Especially after all she'd done for her.

Dr. Woods let him leave, watched him go, staring, even though the elevator doors had closed again. Polly didn't know what to do so she kept quiet, hoping maybe she really had become invisible. They continued downwards in silence, Dr. Woods deep in thought, until the doors opened to the lobby.

Straightening her shoulders, she glanced at Polly, the first sign that the doctor had remembered she was there. "He may think this is finished between us, but it isn't. Not by a long shot." With that, Dr. Layla Woods, looking determined and undeterred, exited the elevator.

Polly stood frozen to the spot, her mind swirling with what she'd just witnessed. It wasn't hatred or anger that fueled them, it was passion. Pure and simple. Those two were meant to be together, and somehow, some way, they'd both have to figure it out. Just before the doors closed Polly rushed out of the elevator and toward the garden exit.

As she ate her dinner, she made a vow. No way would anyone hear a hint of what had gone on in that elevator. Their secret was safe with her, and she hoped Layla was right, that whatever they had going wasn't over by a long shot.

At the end of her shift, completely exhausted, she went to the bathroom to splash some water on her face, hoping to pep herself up for the long subway ride home. Afterwards, she gathered up her belongings from the employee locker room and headed toward the elevator, the last person to leave from the late shift.

A lone silhouette stood at the other end of the hall.

White doctor's coat, broad shoulders, short-cropped hair, unmistakably John. Her heart fluttered at the thought of facing him after several days. He met her at the elevator door.

"What are you still doing here?" he asked.

"Did a double shift."

"Should you be doing that?"

She yawned, and covered her mouth. "No choice these days."

She noticed he festered over that response. He blinked and turned his head as if he had a thing or two to say to her, but had maybe thought better of it.

He looked at his watch. "I don't like the idea of you taking the subway home at this time of night."

"It really isn't about what you like or don't like, now, is it, *Johnny*." Yes, she could be a brat when she wanted to, make that *needed* to. Being pregnant had put her in a whole new frame of mind. Her baby came first, and John wasn't on board with her being pregnant. End of story.

"Let me give you a ride home."

"No way." But, man, oh, man, her feet were tired, and the thought of walking the required blocks just to get to the subway station did seem daunting at almost midnight.

"Look, I had early surgery today so I drove my car. I'm parked next door. Don't be stubborn *and* foolish."

Stubborn? Look who was calling whom stubborn. "Do you have any idea how big the gossip mill is at Angel's? People would have a field day if they saw us leave together." *And then found out soon enough I'm pregnant.*

"Look, dumpling, I don't give a rat's ass what other

people think. Right now, all I want to do is give you a ride home."

"Don't call me dumpling."

"Sorry."

If, and that was a big if, she decided to let John give her a ride home, it wouldn't be because she was giving in to him. No. It would be because she really didn't want to face that long subway ride to the Lower East Side. It had been almost two a.m. before she'd gotten in bed the last time she'd worked a double shift and, being honest, she worried she might fall asleep on the subway and miss her exit.

"Okay."

"Okay you accept my apology or okay you'll let me give you a ride home?"

"I'll take the ride."

He looked surprised, as if she hadn't put up nearly as big a fight as he'd expected.

Ten minutes later she slid onto the smoothest kid leather seat she'd ever seen in a fancy sedan like his. It was soft and cushy, too, and, oh, the headrest was adjusted perfectly to her neck. She touched the button to lower the head of the seat, making it like a lounge chair, and snuggled in after clicking her seat belt.

John didn't say a word, but she could see his cheek lift in that unbalanced smile of his. He'd won. He knew it.

But she was reaping the benefits.

Before he'd even exited the parking structure, she closed her eyes and drifted off to a sweet dream about being curled up on the softest sofa in the world, while the sexiest guy she'd ever met touched her knee and talked to her softly.

CHAPTER SIX

JOHN PARKED THE car, walked around to the other side, opened the passenger door and lifted Polly up and out. She slept sounder than his mother's cat, and only stirred when he pulled her to his chest.

"Shh, go back to sleep," he whispered in her ear, as he motioned with his head to the doorman of his building to let them in.

Marco the doorman gave a deeply inquisitive look but followed orders. John had been a resident in the building for three years now and had never brought a woman home in this condition.

"Drunk," John mouthed to Marco, who gave an affirmative *Aha* nod.

"Park the car in your usual spot?" Marco whispered.

John nodded, knowing his car keys would be left in the parking-garage office where he paid a hefty monthly fee for the privilege of driving and parking in New York City.

He punched the elevator button with his elbow and hoped Polly didn't wake up until he was ready. He'd driven the long way home around Central Park to make sure she'd fallen asleep deeply enough once he'd decided to bring her here.

As he rode the elevator to the ninth floor, he took

the liberty to study her close up—flawless skin, though maybe a little pale, ash-blonde hair with waves that made him want to dig his fingers in every time he saw her. Her thick brown lashes fluttered the tiniest bit under his scrutiny and her nostrils twitched as she breathed softly. She was sweet and tender, and he felt the urge to kiss her.

The elevator door opened, and though it was a bit tricky to unlock his door with one hand while holding Polly with the other, he balanced her on his thigh and succeeded, and had them inside in no time at all. Before anyone on his floor had a chance to wonder what in the world he was doing with a woman in his arms on a Monday night at this late hour. He chuckled inwardly, thinking how they'd never probably even seen him with a woman before, had probably assumed he was gay or celibate.

The condo was dark, but he knew his way around by heart and took her immediately to the guest bedroom, where he carefully laid her on the double bed. She stirred but only to reposition herself on her side. Not wanting to freak her out in case she woke up, which surprisingly she still hadn't, he laid a comforter over her, left the door ajar and went to the kitchen. There, he turned on the light and rummaged around the refrigerator for something to eat.

Three bites into a turkey and Cheddar sandwich he heard the gasp. "Where am I?"

He rushed down the hall to the bedroom. "Don't worry, you're at my place."

"Why am I here?" She came to the door looking groggy and very appealing with mussed-up hair and heavy-lidded eyes.

"You didn't tell me where you lived before you fell

asleep, and you looked so comfortable I didn't have the heart to wake you."

"So you thought you'd make me a prisoner at your house?"

"You're not a prisoner."

"Then you'll take me home?"

"If you insist."

She stood staring, obviously considering his offer. Maybe she needed some convincing.

"Look, I was thinking of your best interests. I've got the guest bedroom and you'll get a good night's sleep, then I'll take you home in the morning."

"I don't have to work tomorrow because I did the double shift."

"That's fine."

"Don't you have to be at work?"

"Not until nine. It's my clinic day."

"So you'll take me home before you go to work?"

He nodded.

She leaned against the doorframe looking drowsy and too tired to put up a fight. "Where's your bathroom, please?"

He gestured with his forehead towards the door down the hall, then took another bite of sandwich.

On her way back to the guest room she slowed down by the kitchen and gave him a suspicious glance. "Don't get any ideas about sneaking into that room tonight." She pointed to the guest room.

"I won't."

"Because what we did was a one-time deal."

He didn't bother to swallow his bite of sandwich. "By my count, that was a three-time deal."

Obviously too tired to put up a fight, she tossed him an aggravated look then went inside the guest room and closed the door. At least she didn't lock it. He took the last bite of sandwich and decided he'd got a kick out of riling her. Come to think of it, there was a lot about Polly he got a kick out of. Now, if there was only a way to get her back into his life on much better terms.

Early the next morning, John had a full breakfast prepared by the time he tapped on her door and woke her up. She rolled out of the room, stretching and yawning and looking even more inviting than she had the night before.

"What time is it?" she asked.

"Seven. Have some coffee. It's decaf," he said, before she could protest. Somehow he knew she'd take good care of the pregnancy. "I've scrambled some eggs and there's fresh OJ over there. Do you like wheat or sourdough toast?"

"Wheat," she said, before closing the bathroom door.

The fact that she didn't throw a hissy fit or make a major protest about getting home right this minute gave him hope, and that notion made him smile. Maybe she was back to being that people-pleaser he liked so much, though the feisty version of Polly definitely had its merits. He smiled and pushed some perfectly scrambled eggs onto a second plate then sprinkled some finely grated Cheddar cheese on top.

They sat on bar stools in companionable silence while they ate at his granite counter.

"Tastes good," she said, eating a second piece of toast slathered with blackberry jam.

"You're eating for two now, right?"

He'd named the elephant in the room, and she took her time to respond. "I don't need you to remind me." Her gaze was brief and filled with icy-blue warning.

"I want to be a part of this pregnancy, Polly."

"That's not the impression I got when I told you about it."

"I was in shock."

"You wanted nothing to do with me or this pregnancy. You tried to pay me off, as if I'd go away and never mention another word about it."

He reached for her hand and squeezed. "I didn't mean it to come off that way. I wanted you to know you weren't in it alone, and that you didn't have to worry about money. That's all."

She dropped her gaze toward her lap. "We're not for sale."

If that was the metaphor she wanted to run with, he'd play along. "Look at it from my perspective." He pointed to her stomach. "There's prime real estate inside there, and though you may be the landlord, I own half of it."

She made a face at him. "Have you always been this romantic?"

He shrugged. "It's a gift."

"You don't have the right to make it all neat and tidy like that. Like a business deal." Polly shoved another bite of egg into her mouth and stared straight ahead. Once she'd swallowed, she leveled a serious gaze at him. "I don't have a clue what your issues are, but since I believe you do need to be there for this baby I'll generously consider whatever part of 'being there for this pregnancy' you think you can handle."

He grinned. That was the people-pleasing Polly he knew. "Good. For starters, I intend to go to all obstetric appointments with you."

Her eyebrows dropped and furrowed. "That's a very private thing."

"And one doesn't wind up pregnant by not doing

a few *very private* things with the father of the baby, does one?"

She sighed. "Okay, you can come to the OB appointments."

"And you should let me cook for you at least twice a week."

"You cook?"

"What do you call these scrambled eggs?"

"A six-year-old can scramble eggs, Johnny."

She'd called him Johnny again, and he'd consider it progress. "I happen to be a good cook, and I want to make sure you get a balanced diet."

"Look, I may have gotten knocked up with little effort but I am not an idiot. I know how to eat healthily."

"There was a *lot* of effort involved in you getting pregnant, as I recall, and for the record you didn't get 'knocked up', as you so poetically put it, on your own."

Silence stretched on for a few seconds while he regrouped. How long would he have to keep pointing out to her that she didn't have to be in this alone? If he didn't handle things right this time, he could blow it all for good.

"I was on birth-control pills," she said. "I swear I was, but I'd taken antibiotics a few weeks back for a sinus infection."

"I see." He understood perfectly what she was getting at, she didn't want him to think she'd set him up. Antibiotics could interfere with birth control pills' potency and effect for a couple of weeks after use, enough to make a woman potentially vulnerable to pregnancy. Under the circumstances, and without added protection, which they'd completely blown off that night, pregnancy wasn't out of the question. Polly and her baby onboard were living proof.

John ate the remainder of his breakfast vigorously. The real question was, though, why hadn't she thought about that when they'd made love? Ah, hell, why hadn't *he* thought about anything but how much he'd wanted her that night? There was no point in making this a blame game. What was done was done. They'd had sex, hot sex, and made a baby.

Though there was no way on earth he could invest emotionally in the pregnancy, or be a proper father, he could at least be an ally for Polly during a time when she would definitely need a friend. As for after the pregnancy? He downed the last of his orange juice. Well, he was content to take it one step at a time for now, and she'd just have to understand.

"So I'll wait for you at the hospital parking lot on Thursday when you get off work, and take you to your appointment."

"Okay." She sounded like a teenager who'd given up on getting out of a major book report. "But can you take me home now? I'd really like to shower."

"Of course."

On Thursday, Polly ran a little late after change-of-shift report and had to run-walk to meet John at the car. He'd had the car brought up to the entrance and leaned against his silver sedan, checking his watch as she jogged his way.

"Sorry! We had some late admits and I couldn't just dump and run."

"I've already called the doctor's office and let them know we may be a little late. I'll drop you off in front then park."

"Great. Thanks." She fixed the flying strands of hair around her face, knowing her skin was probably shiny from working hard all day and that her colored lip gloss had long ago been chewed off. "I really appreciate it."

"It's the least I can do."

The least he could do, was that how he looked at it? Was he only trying to get away with doing the bare minimum so as not to come off as a deadbeat? Boy, had she been there and done that with her aunts and uncles after her mother had died. Every part of that equation made her skin crawl, yet here she was, riding in John Griffin's fancy car on her way to the doctor's appointment he'd arranged. She was sick of people going through the motions on her behalf, but that seemed to be the repetitious hand life had dealt her. Resigned, she'd just have to make the best of it this time, not for her but for her baby's sake.

Dr. Bernstein's nurse was ready for her the minute she walked in and whisked her into one of the examination rooms in the glamorous medical suite. She had no intention of letting John in on the actual examination.

The doctor looked to be around John's age and had gentle hands and an affable personality. He looked intently into her eyes as she explained her side of the pregnancy, and she believed him when he promised to keep her and the baby healthy and happy for the next eight and a half months.

"You can get dressed then meet me in my office," he said on his way out the door after the thorough examination.

Polly suffered a surprise when she entered Dr. Bernstein's office only to find John already sitting there, chatting amicably with "Geoff", as he called him. The moment Polly stepped inside the conversation stopped and John shot up. He reached over and pulled out the chair next to him so she could sit. She'd give him points for always being a gentleman.

"Polly," Dr. "Geoff" started right in, "you are a healthy young woman, and at this early stage in the process I'd say you're going to do well. Your uterus and cervix look good, the pregnancy is implanted securely in your uterus lining, and your pelvic cradle should handle the body changes just fine. I want to get some baseline lab work done for you and start you on prenatal vitamins. In a couple of weeks we'll do an ultrasound." He scribbled on a prescription pad, ripped it off and handed it to her, then sat back in his chair and steepled his fingers. "Do you have any questions?"

"My due date?"

"Right. My calculations show March twenty-eighth, give or take a day or two."

The skin on her shoulders and arms prickled. Some-how, this actual date of birth made everything come into focus. It was real. She'd have a baby and be a mom be-ginning March twenty-eighth. John must have noticed her emotional reaction when he put his arm around her shoulders and tugged her close. She couldn't help the brimming tears. She was going to be a mother in eight short months from now. Only because the long and stressful day had caught up with her, and she needed it right this moment, she accepted John's comfort as she buried her weeping eyes on his shoulder.

Back at the car, John grinned at her as he let her in the passenger side. "You agreed to let me fix you din-ner twice a week, and I thought tonight would be a good time to get that routine rolling."

"You don't even know if I have food allergies or anything." She'd recovered from the emotional high in the doctor's office and had pulled up her guard again.

"Chicken tetrazzini with wholegrain noodles and a garden salad."

Her mouth watered at the description. "I hate onions. Does it have onions?"

"Not now. I hope you like garlic, though."

She bobbed her head as she slid inside the car. Hating having to hold back all her excitement about being pregnant, she tightened her jaw and ground her teeth for most of the ride back to John's condo.

Marco the doorman gave her and John a knowing nod when they walked inside, and it made her pause. Had she ever seen him before? The small but tasteful lobby gave her the impression that well-off, long-time New Yorkers lived in the building. What a difference from her turn-of-the-century walk-up.

Though John had overall masculine flair in his taste in interior design, a maroon leather couch and chair with glass and chrome tables got her attention, and across the room a surprising floral-upholstered over-stuffed chair and ottoman looked beyond inviting.

"Have a seat," he said, gesturing to the living room that flowed naturally into his kitchen. "You need to rest as often as you can." He tossed her the newspaper he'd just sorted out of his pile of mail. "Read this while I get cooking."

"Don't be so bossy." At a little after five o'clock she was hungry and more than ready to eat, and decided not to give him a hard time, so she did what she was told and put her feet up, shaking out the newspaper and reading the headlines of the day, all of which were depressing.

She surreptitiously kept track of him while he cooked. He wore khaki slacks that fit in all the right places and a pale blue shirt. He'd removed the tie while he'd shuffled through his mail, and the open-collar look held her interest longer than she'd wanted. But most of all what kept her riveted to watching John was how he genuinely seemed to enjoy cooking. She liked discovering that about him.

He ran a tidy kitchen and was very comfortable in it, like cooking was a less sterile version of surgery. She thought of her living arrangement and the tiny outdated appliances she shared. What she'd give to have such a gorgeous modern kitchen at her fingertips. The comfort of the chair and the simple dream of living in a place like John's soon had her closing her suddenly weary eyes…

"Dinner's ready!"

Polly sat bolt upright. What time was it? She glanced at her watch. Six o'clock. She'd taken a forty-minute nap. The hint of garlic, chicken and freshly drained pasta weaving their way from the kitchen and up her nostrils was heavenly. "Give me a sec to wash up, okay?"

"Of course." He whistled while he set plates and flatware on the bistro-sized table in the corner of the kitchen, and she stopped a couple of moments to enjoy the sight.

The food smelled fantastic and her taste buds went into overdrive, looking forward to the meal as she hurried down the hall to wash her hands.

He hadn't lied. John Griffin was a darned fine cook. Every mouthful sent jets of pleasure through her gastronomic senses. She could get used to these twice-a-week meals, maybe bargain for a third as time went on. Piecemeal, really, since that was all he was offering in the way of getting involved in the pregnancy. Far be it from her to want to ruin a delicious dinner, but really was that the best the man could offer? She continued to eat with a disappointed outlook.

After a few bites John put his fork down and cast a pressing gaze at her. She wasn't about to stop eating, but the daunting stare did slow her down a bit.

"I want you to know that I liked you right off. You know, that first week you came to Angel's. I, or we, did something crazy and out of character, and now we've been thrown together in some pretty astounding circumstances."

She wanted to ask him how long he'd practiced the speech, but decided, as he was finally opening up, not to be a smart-aleck.

He cleared his throat. "What I'm getting at is I know you're disappointed in me. I'm only skirting around the perimeter of our predicament."

She started to protest his calling her pregnancy a predicament, but when she opened her mouth he raised his voice a pre-emptive notch. "I don't think any guy would know how to handle it perfectly, but I'm not making excuses for myself. I'm just being honest with you, because I think you deserve it."

He got up, refilled his water glass, took a long draw and sat back down. "There's something you need to know about me. Maybe it will explain why I'm not all balloons and bubbles over your pregnancy."

Sensing his earnestness, she put her fork down and gave him her total attention. "Go ahead, John."

As if the words strangled and fought in his throat, John's pained expression made Polly brace for what he was about to say.

"I don't even know if I told you that I used to be married. Happily married for two years. My wife, Lisa, was a financial adviser." His voice clogged and he stopped every sentence or two to clear it. "Anyway, we were happy because she'd just found out she was pregnant."

The heavy foreshadowing made the gourmet meal in Polly's stomach suddenly feel like a large lump of paper maché. John talked to the table rather than engage her eyes.

"We'd stayed up late, planning, all excited about our baby, how our lives would change." He had to clear that stubborn lump in his throat again. His nose ran and he wiped it with his paper napkin. Instinctively, the hair on Polly's arms rose and John's profile grew blurry.

"We were going to tell my parents over dinner that night. I kissed her goodbye that morning and she went to work on the twenty-second floor of the World Trade Center on September eleventh."

Chills rolled over Polly's skin. Tears broke free from her eyes and she realized the implication of that fateful day. She'd been a high-school student at the time, eating breakfast and listening to the kitchen radio when she'd heard the news report. She grabbed John's knotted fist and squeezed tight. Oh, God, he didn't need to say one more word. She understood. He'd lost everything he loved and held dear on one historic day.

Polly got up from her seat and circled around John, banding her arms around his chest as she cuddled him from behind. He sat stoic, like the rock of Gibraltar he'd tricked himself into becoming—for survival's sake, she was sure, she understood that now. Bleeding emotionally for his loss, she stayed with him wrapped in her arms for several long moments as she mulled over their circumstances. She was willing to give him a pass for now, for not committing to their child beyond the neat and tidy logistics of appointments, well-prepared dinners, and finances.

Slowly, as she stood hunched over, holding him, a tiny thought wiggled and snaked its way clear of her emotional landslide on John's behalf. The thought gained power and implanted itself in the center of her head. *That was twelve years ago.* Was John determined to keep his life stagnant and take the loss to his grave? More importantly, would Lisa want that for him?

They may have made love under unusual circumstances, but something bigger than both of them had come out of it. They'd made a baby. He could never get his wife or child back, but she and John had made a little life that was growing inside her. A baby with a birth date. March twenty-eighth.

It was Polly's turn to clear her thickened throat. "John, please don't get me wrong, I realize how horrific your loss was. But twelve years have passed, and that's no excuse for abandoning your responsibility to *this* child." She stood straight and placed her hand on her currently flat abdomen, one hand anchored to his shoulder. "This baby needs you now. You're the father."

He sat staring at his plate rather than acknowledge her, and when she'd given up on him answering she dropped her hands from his shoulder and her stomach and cleared the dishes from the table.

"I'll take care of that," he said, belatedly.

"No, this is my way of thanking you for a great meal." As long as he held onto the past, she'd never have a chance to really get to know him.

John removed the remaining dishes and joined her at the sink. Together they worked in silence, cleaning the kitchen.

"Can you take me home now, please?" she asked, once everything was done.

"Sure."

Noncommittal seemed to be all the man could offer, and his history explained why, but that definitely wasn't something she'd settle for, and John really did need to let go of the past.

John watched Polly from across the kitchen. Her petite frame looked good in anything she wore, which happened to be hospital scrubs. She was right about so many years having gone by, he knew. He couldn't argue with the logic of being held captive by a time capsule, but the habit had become so deeply rooted into his being that he couldn't seem to break free. He'd been one of the first responders at the scene and to this day he had flashbacks of treating the injured and mangled, of staring into the faces of the dead, while desperate to find his wife. He'd taken risks amongst the falling debris and rubble searching for Lisa, but it had all been fruitless. She'd died and taken most of him with her. To this day he questioned why he'd lived and she hadn't.

When Polly had gathered her things, he got his keys and they headed for the elevator.

An hour later, due to heavy traffic conditions, when John dropped Polly off at her century-old building on the Lower East Side, a crazy idea popped into his head. She was the one accusing him of abandoning his responsibility to the child. She'd probably never agree to it but, what the hell, when the time was right, he'd make his pitch.

He'd double-parked and watched while she climbed the stoop stairs and buzzed herself into the building. The thought of her surviving during the long hot summer while being pregnant and living in the ancient brownstone walk-up didn't sit well. He couldn't offer his heart to a stranger, but he owed her the common decency of making sure she was comfortable and cared for.

Patience, John, give her some time to realize how hard things will get on her own, then you can make her the offer she can't refuse.

CHAPTER SEVEN

FRIDAY MORNING POLLY was measuring out liquid antibiotics at the medicine station for the three-year-old toddler in Room Twelve B when John appeared in her peripheral vision.

He pushed a small brown bag her way. "Here."

"What's this?"

"Your lunch," he said, already walking away.

"I made my own lunch."

"Save it for tomorrow. You'll like this better."

"How do you know that? Maybe I've been craving peanut butter and jelly all day. Maybe I've been dreaming about my home-made lunch since breakfast." When had she reverted to being a contrary teenager again? Could it be the hormones?

He stopped, turned and flashed that slanting smile, his dark eyes reminding her of milk-chocolate chips. Beneath his knee-length doctor's coat he wore a white shirt and blue silk tie, looking dressier than usual. She inhaled, the savory scent coming from the bag already making her mouth water. Something warm and spicy awaited her, thanks to Dr. Griffin, the father of her baby.

He'd gone out of his way to bring this to her so the least she could do was be grateful.

She mouthed, "Thank you". He dipped his head and

walked away. Truth was, she could easily get used to him catering for her, and wondered how abruptly it would end once she had the baby. She glanced around, noticing Brooke and Rafael giving her odd looks. Oh, man, what must they think? The last thing she needed was to get picked up for the gossip grapevine like that poor Dr. Woods and the neurosurgeon, Dr. Rodriguez. Thank goodness Janetta didn't work the day shift.

After finishing the obviously home-made minestrone soup with spinach and chicken meatballs, Polly found at the bottom of the lunch bag a large peanut-butter cookie with a note hidden behind it.

Meet me for an early dinner at Giovanni's to-night? See you there at five.

How could he be so confident she'd come running just because he'd told her to? She went back to work determined to blow him off. Let him sit there and wait for her to show up. She may be pregnant, but she was darned sure not to be taken for granted because of it.

As the afternoon wore on, she prepared a teenage soccer player for surgery on his left knee and right shoulder. She'd given him his pre-op medicine and shot and stayed close by until the transportation clerk could take him to the operating room. As his eyelids grew heavy and he dozed off, she thought about John and his sexy blue silk tie and that off-balance but charming smile. Did she really want to play games with him? He'd asked her to dinner, had seemed sincere enough, and she had no reason not to go, so why stand him up?

The man had been to hell and back over the past twelve years. Here he was getting a little sparkle in his eyes again, and the last thing she should do was give him a hard time. It wasn't in her nature to play games with men anyway. Besides, in her dating life the guys had always been much better at game-playing than she could ever compete with.

No, after work she'd take her time and freshen up then walk over to Giovanni's for another dinner with John. Memories of what had happened after the last time they'd eaten there made her lose her step but not stumble. She'd make sure it didn't happen again, and maybe she'd ask him to drive her home, just to make sure. Besides, lately the fumes in the subway made her feel nauseous.

To her surprise, John was already there, waiting, when she arrived. He'd ordered bottled water instead of Chianti, too, which was sitting on the table. He stood when he saw her, and the smile he gave was definitely genuine. So was the warm feeling inside when she smiled back at him. Without his doctor's jacket she could see his solid, football-player physique, and it spawned a quick flash of being naked in his arms and near bliss.

"If you like shrimp, I recommend the scampi," he said, sitting down after she'd shaken the sexy thought from her mind and taken her seat.

"So much for idle conversation. You say dinner. You mean dinner." She picked up the menu and scanned the specials.

"I'm sorry, is there something you'd like to talk about?"

She screwed up her face. "No. It's just, well, customary when meeting someone for dinner to start off with small talk like 'Hi, how was your day?' or something before getting right down to ordering."

"Sorry. I have an administrative meeting at seven."

"On a Friday night?" There went her chance for a ride home. "So why'd you invite me here, then?" If he wanted to get right down to business, so could she.

He poured both of them a glass of the sparkling bottled water then took a drink of his. "I want you to move in with me."

She almost spit her water right into his face, but instead she swallowed it wrong and coughed. He patted her back, looking concerned. She coughed and hacked for several more seconds, eyes bugging out, feeling embarrassed about how she must look. He looked on, earnestly trying to figure out how to help her. After she settled down she said, "You what?"

"You heard me right. I've been thinking about this and as we're having this baby together, it's the least I can do."

That warm something or other she'd felt momentarily when she'd first walked in and seen him smiling at her turned to ice. "The least you can do? Well, how kind of you, sir. Thank you for the magnanimous crumb." She stood, fully intending to leave. "As far as I'm concerned, you can take that crumb and shove it!" With the room melting down to nothing as her anger overtook every cell in her body, she stomped towards the exit. Before she made it to the street, a big, strong hand grabbed her arm.

"Hold on, hothead."

She yanked back her arm and kept moving, now outside the restaurant. He followed close behind. "Leave me alone. You're a jerk."

He managed to get in front of her, planted both hands on her arms and forced her to stop and look at him. "I know I'm a jerk. I can't figure out how not to be a jerk *or* how to handle this thing. Give me a break, will you? I'm trying. I want to do what's right, okay?"

The fury rumbling through her chest lost strength with each of his sentences. The man was being painfully honest, how refreshing, and she could see it in his tense yet imploring eyes. She blinked then glanced at the darkening sky. She'd made a point to never depend on anyone after the day she'd turned eighteen. Being a child at the mercy of uninterested aunts and uncles had been the most painful part of her life. She couldn't allow herself to depend on John, though she sure could use his help for a while.

Was it wise to get more deeply involved with someone she barely knew? No. Especially since she'd had a fierce crush on John until everything had gone to hell in a handbasket with this surprise pregnancy.

"Well?" John said, confusion with a touch of impatience in his stare.

"I'm thinking. Can't you give me a minute?" She glanced at him, reinforcing his jerk status, then went back to staring at the sky. She didn't know what the heck she wanted from John, yet he was offering to open his home to her. It wasn't all about herself any more. Nope. She had a baby to think about. Was there anything wrong with testing the waters where John was concerned? She wouldn't dare get her hopes up or anything, but maybe for a while staying with John in a strictly platonic way could be useful for both her and her baby.

"Okay."

He lightened his hold. "Okay what? You'll give me a break?"

"I'll move in." Why mess around with pretenses. She was knocked up. He was the father. She hated where she lived, and he'd just offered her a room in his homey condo—a beautiful apartment in a gorgeous part of the city. Why be coy?

"Just like that, you change your mind. You're ready to move in?"

"Yes. I'll try it out for a week, see how things go. It will depend on whether or not we're compatible. In a strictly platonic way. Got it?"

His shocked expression quickly turned to happy, then ricocheted to suspicious. "Whatever you say, dumpling."

She slowly shook her head. Even if it was a crumb, he'd offered to help, and though she'd been prepared to make it through this pregnancy on her own, she appreciated his gesture, knowing it was way out of his comfort zone. How often in her life had she been invited into a home? Why not take advantage of a win-win situation? A nice place to live. Good food prepared in a kitchen without grease stains everywhere. A roomy bathroom without leaky faucets, mildew, and cracked tile. She could walk to work. Take walks by the East River in the evenings. If she got sick there'd be a doctor in the house.

He tugged on his earlobe, a combination of relief and shock registering on his face. "Okay, then. It's settled. One week with the option to make it longer, okay?"

"Sweet."

"Now will you have the scampi?"

Against her will a laugh escaped her lips. "Sure, why not?" He guided her back into the restaurant. "It isn't every day a girl gets a proposition she can't refuse, *plus* a shrimp dinner."

He ran his hand over his short hair. "Yeah, well, it didn't come out the way I'd practiced."

She sputtered another laugh. "You practiced that?"

"Like I said…" He pulled out the chair so she could sit back down.

It did her heart good to see a grown man and skilled orthopedic surgeon, department head like John Griffin fumble and stumble over his words and actions because of her. Maybe she and the baby did mean something to him. *Don't let yourself go there. He's got a lot of proving to do first.*

She sat down and took another sip of water. There was only one way to find out if the man cared about her or not, and under these challenging and unusual circumstances she'd made a snap decision to find out.

By moving in for a week.

Saturday afternoon, John helped Polly move out of her tiny rented room and managed to fit everything in the trunk and back seat of his car. She'd decided to bring everything so she wouldn't have to keep running back to the old place for this or that as the need arose. Besides, there wasn't that much and why leave anything for Mrs. Goldman to snoop through while she was gone?

When she assessed all her worldly belongings, it made her heart feel a little heavier in her chest. The only precious item was a small cherry-wood jewelry box that had belonged to her mother. In it was a delicate gold locket with an enameled cover. It was heart shaped and opened to her mother's picture on one side and Polly's on the other. Thinking about her single cherished item from twenty-one years ago made her wonder what object John still treasured from Lisa.

Back at the apartment, she would set the boundaries right off—she intended to stay in his guest room rather than share his bed. Until he could move on from his past, there was no point in trying for a real relationship with John. It kind of hurt her feelings when he didn't put up a fight about their sleeping arrangements, but she let those thoughts pass.

For a reputed grumpy old department head, John had been polite and helpful the whole weekend, and she began to see the balloon-twisting, cast-signing side of him. The man all the kids on the orthopedic ward adored. He made coffee in the morning and breakfast after that. Before she could offer to make lunch, he beat her to it. Being in his home, he was more relaxed and extremely considerate about making her feel welcome. If only the rest of the staff could see through his shield, but children seemed to have that special gift of looking into the true heart of a person. As for her, she was happy for the new glimpse of him.

On Sunday afternoon John took her on a walking tour of his neighborhood, which was another way of making her feel welcome. Delighted to find a yarn shop, she talked him into letting her go inside. Not in the least bit interested, he waited outside, chatting with a neighbor he'd run into, and she made her purchase quickly, embarrassed to let him see what she'd bought. It was silly, she knew, but she hadn't knitted in a long time and, well, she was pregnant! She kept the items in a brown bag and his lack of interest made it easy to drop the subject so on they walked through the amazing and upscale neighbourhood of Sutton Place.

They ended the tour on a bench at a small park overlooking the East River. How different this part of town was from the Lower East Side. From a money standpoint, John lived a charmed life, but she knew the whole story—he was alone and hurting. Terribly alone. Even though it seemed he was the one with all the advantages, she knew she could bring something sorely missing into his life. Maybe, with this pregnancy, she could help him experience joy again.

As she stared at the Queensboro Bridge arching across the river, she hoped for any tiny miracle that could open John's heart again. If an unexpected pregnancy was what it would take to shake some life back into him, so be it.

Deep in thought, she jumped when he took her hand. "What do you say we head for home?"

Home? Did she really and finally have a home?

"I thought I'd make pasta for dinner tonight."

So far he'd cooked all the meals. "Why don't you let me cook tonight?"

"Let me take care of you."

Polly couldn't let herself dream too much. All the years she'd never let herself get too comfortable wherever she was staying had trained her to take nothing for granted. If she got swept up in this little fantasy of having a home, it would hurt that much more when reality kicked in, and in her life reality always stepped in.

"Besides, you're my guest. It's my job to make you feel at home."

So she was just a guest. She really needed to keep that in mind. She may as well let him wait on her, and while he made the spaghetti sauce she'd start her knitting project.

By Monday, Polly didn't know how the hospital radar had picked it up so fast but she'd noticed odd glances and hushed conversations that stopped abruptly whenever she got near. It wasn't in her nature to be paranoid, but she was beginning to wonder if someone had been spying on her and John over the weekend.

During lunch, while eating another carefully prepared meal by John, she cornered Darren and grilled him. "Is something going on I don't know about?"

"I think I should be asking you that," he said, taking a huge bite of an Italian lunchmeat sandwich.

"What's everyone whispering about?" She decided to continue to play dumb.

"We're all wondering exactly when you and Dr. Griffin found the time to become a couple. That's all."

"We're not a couple."

"You're not. A couple."

She thinned her lips and shook her head.

"Who made that lunch for you?" He used his sandwich to point at her wholewheat bread, sliced chicken with avocado and sprouts sandwich.

She thought about lying but that wasn't in her nature. "John—I mean Dr. Griffin did." She didn't want to come clean until she cleared it with John.

"And who'd you walk into work with this morning?

In a month or two it would be apparent enough that she was pregnant, but until then why rush to tell everyone? "I got kicked out of my apartment and Dr. Griffin said I could use his guest room until I found something else." Okay, it was a half-lie, but she didn't have to spill the beans about being pregnant just yet.

Darren leveled her with a you-can't-fool-me glare. "His guest room. Uh-huh."

She leaned forward and got in his face. "Yes, uh-huh, his guest room. And I'd appreciate it if you kept everything I've told you to yourself, Darren."

He stared into her eyes, as if assessing how serious she was, then seemed to make his decision. "My lips are sealed," he said, immediately taking another huge bite of sandwich.

Realizing her personal business would sooner or later

become a juicy story for workplace gossip made her feel queasy. She'd only managed to eat half of her own sandwich but had already lost her appetite.

The next morning Polly moaned over the bathroom toilet, experiencing her first full-fledged bout of morning sickness. Lord, how would she be able to go to work feeling as though she stood on the ledge of losing it all, just waiting for someone or something to nudge her over?

"Breakfast is ready!" John called from the kitchen.

Oh, God, that was all it took. She hurled.

"I'm not hungry." She'd come up for air and managed to call back between bouts.

A few seconds later determined footsteps down the hardwood hallway grew closer. He tapped on the bathroom door. "You okay?"

"If you call being sick to your stomach okay, then I'm peachy."

"Morning sickness?"

She moaned instead of replied.

He waited outside while she cleaned up, rinsed out her mouth and opened the bathroom door. "I think if you eat some dry cereal or saltine crackers before you get out of bed tomorrow, it might help."

The thought of eating anything made her stomach clench in preparation for losing more of its contents. She twitched her nose and put her hand over her mouth. "I'm sorry, but your cologne is making me more nauseous."

"I'll wash it off," he said, without giving it a second thought.

A few minutes later he was at her bedroom door with a plastic bag in his hand. "You might think this is crazy, but it used to help Lisa." He handed her the bag filled with lemon slices. "It helps to smell citrus or suck on peppermint if odors set off your nausea." He handed her a roll of peppermints. "You can squeeze the lemon into water, too. Oh, and I can get some bottled fruit juice and make popsicles for you to suck on so you won't get dehydrated."

She wanted more than anything to be grateful for the sweet gesture, but everything he said had to do with eating, and her nausea grew worse and worse. She walked backwards toward the bathroom, listening to him and bobbing her head, then quickly closed the door.

"I'll tell Brooke you're not coming in today. You can't go to work like this."

"I don't have sick leave yet. I won't get paid."

"That's the last thing you need to worry about. I'll handle it," he said, walking way.

And handle it he did. From the bathroom she could hear him all the way down the hall.

"Brooke? It's Dr. Griffin. Listen, Polly is having morning sickness and needs to miss work today. How do I know?"

Obviously, John hadn't thought through all the ramifications of him calling in sick on Polly's behalf. Now what would he do?

"Well, uh. Listen, this is strictly confidential. She's staying with me for now. Just keep that between you and me, okay?"

Polly moaned. Didn't he have a clue? The effect of his innocent honesty showed how out of touch he was with his own staff, and the phone call, coupled with what she'd already let slip with Darren, was nothing short of a department-wide gossip memo announcing they now lived together and she was pregnant with his baby.

So much for keeping the cat in the bag a bit longer.

As if feeling sick to her stomach wasn't enough, the realization that soon everyone at work would know her personal business sent her head right back into the bowl.

John wasn't sure he'd ever get used to the quick glances and whispers whenever he did rounds on the orthopedic ward, so he chose to ignore them. He did, however, have to admit that never in a million years would he expect his name to be linked to a sweet small-town girl like Polly Seymour.

Having her living with him hadn't taken nearly as much getting used to as he'd assumed he'd need. She was quiet and calm, and sometimes he barely knew she was there, especially when she went to her room and did whatever she did after dinner until she went to bed. He wished she'd come out of her room more often and spend time with him.

He sensed she didn't want to be any more of an imposition than she assumed she was. Truth was, she wasn't an imposition at all. He liked having her there, having someone to cook for and look after. Someone to talk things over with. He liked her gentle, sunny nature, too. He even got a kick out of the twangy country music she liked to listen to on the radio in her room.

His apartment had never seemed more like a home.

John walked toward a fourteen-year-old boy's room to talk with the mother about Thursday's scheduled knee and ankle repair. The young teen, named Eric Caldera, had injured it playing in the dark at summer camp in Maine. It would be a long procedure and involve pins and plates and possibly even a bone graft. He wouldn't know exactly how extensive the repair would be until he started surgery.

Eric's parents were estranged, making all consultations tricky. The father had visitation rights with Eric, but the mother preferred never to be in the same room with him. Cases like these at Angel's required social services to step in to work out the details so all involved, especially the patient, could have their wishes met. After seeing the mother, who wouldn't leave her son's bedside, he'd give a call to the father and repeat everything he'd said to the mother. It might be double work, but he believed both parents deserved to be informed.

On his way into the room his gaze met and held Polly's. Something odd fizzed through his chest, and he winked at her. Her sky-blue eyes got wide and she covered with her hand the smile threatening to burst free. He liked taking her by surprise...like that night they'd made love.

She looked cute in her brightly colored top covered in cartoon angels on clouds and those bright pink scrub pants. Pretty in pink. Yeah, his new roommate was pretty in pink.

Entering the patient room, his smile was wide. Well, wide by John Griffin's standards, anyway, because he had something special to look forward to. Later today he'd accompany Polly for her first ultrasound at Geoff's office.

Standing beside the procedure table in the darkened ultrasonographer's room, John was as interested as Polly in seeing the first view of their baby. An ultrasound this early in the game wasn't called for, but more than anything John wanted to make sure the pregnancy was well implanted.

Having followed the preparation orders to a T, Polly

had been dancing around the waiting room, swearing she'd wet herself if they didn't take her in soon. He'd laughed at her antics, wishing he could help her get comfortable some way, but knew this was totally out of his realm of expertise.

Polly lay on the table with a sheet over her abdomen, looking excited yet in pain from her extra-full bladder. When the tech pulled back the sheet and squirted the cold conducting gel on her belly, she glanced at him, raised her shoulders and grimaced, letting out a tiny squeal. How could that flat abdomen possibly house a baby? John wondered. He hadn't seen her smooth ivory skin since the night they'd been together, and his re-action of longing to touch her surprised him. But now was not the time or place to get hot for his live-in nurse.

He'd pulled strings to have the ultrasound this early along in the pregnancy. After all, it had been barely five weeks since she'd gotten pregnant, the baby's heart wouldn't even be completely formed or beating yet, but Geoff was more than happy to accommodate them.

"We'll only be able to see the gestational sac," the sonographer said as she moved the transducer back and forth over Polly's taut skin.

Polly reached out and on reflex John took her hand. She squeezed, and he mindlessly ran his thumb back and forth over her icy fingers. He wanted to kiss her, right there in front of the tech. He didn't give a damn. He wanted to kiss her.

But he didn't, choosing instead to squeeze back on her hand when the fan-shaped image of Polly's uterus first appeared on the monitor.

"There it is," the tech said. "That's the gestational sac. Oh, and see that tiny thing? About the size of an orange seed? That's the embryo."

John had to squint to see it, but it was there. Their baby. The hair on his arms rose as assorted feelings of awe and joy along with an ancient ache rolled through him. He was definitely going to be a father, and he remembered exactly how he'd felt when Lisa had told him the news all those years ago.

"Oh, my gosh, look at that, Johnny," Polly said on gust of breath.

Warmth enveloped him, reaching through layers of protection to the deepest part of his heart as he glanced first at the screen then into the face of an angel. His angel, who'd brought life back into his lonely existence.

"Looks like we're really having a baby, dumpling."

The look she returned, full of wonder, joy, and excitement, was worth every single one of those twelve barren years.

John took Polly to a restaurant in Central Park for dinner on the balmy August evening. Outside on the deck they watched swans and ducks, rowboats, and even a gondola drift by as she sipped lemonade. She ordered hazelnut-crusted East Coast halibut with asparagus, cherry tomatoes, mushrooms and some kind of divine vinaigrette, grateful her morning sickness always seemed to wane by early afternoons. He went for a curry with shrimp and scallops.

As they ate, things loosened up between them. Even more incredibly, John opened up to her about his family without Polly prodding him first.

"My sister Dana is going to be floored when she finds out I'm going to be a father."

"Is she close by?"

He shook his head. "She lives in Rhode Island. She's been on my butt to get married again for years." His eyes drifted away momentarily and Polly wondered what he was thinking. Certainly he wasn't thinking about marrying her.

"Uh, Johnny, we hardly know each other. Aren't we going to just wait and see how things work out?"

He pulled back from his brief mental absence. "Oh, of course. I was just thinking back to when I lost Lisa and how important Dana was in helping me get by. My mom and dad were as devastated as I was and, well Dana was this rock for all of us."

"She sounds like a great sister. I always wished I'd had a sister or brother."

"We hated each other growing up, but now we're like this." He crossed his fingers. "First thing every summer I give her and her husband, Jerome, a break by taking my nephews camping."

"That sounds fun. Where did you go this year?"

"Maine. Acadia National Park."

"I've never been."

"You've got to go. It's beautiful."

There were so many places she'd never seen. Dare she dream of having someone to travel with and share special moments? Her mind drifted far away to the land of dreams come true, and she hadn't a clue how long she stayed there but most of her dinner had been eaten and John was talking about his parents when she checked back in.

"My parents eat dinner at four-thirty every day in Florida. They drive around in these electric carts like everyone else in the retirement community, it's the funniest thing. I took my life in my hands when I visited last year and insisted on walking around the place. They need some kind of signage that says '*Pedestrians Be-*

ware'! I nearly got sideswiped twice." He gave that genuine cockeyed smile she'd come to adore.

Polly laughed, imagining John dodging electric carts in some distant retirement community.

When dessert came, she ventured into uncharted waters. "Do you think it's too early to think about names?"

"Mort," he said. "I like Mort." When John let down his guard he had natural deadpan humor. At least, she hoped he was being funny about this name business.

She threw a leftover piece of bread at him. "No way, dude." The impish expression on his face gave him away.

"Hey, my favorite uncle was named Mortimer." Such a tease John was.

"What do you think about Sterling?"

"It's okay, but only if I can call him Mort for short."

She rolled her eyes and glanced at the full moon hanging in the sky. Mr. Sterling had been her favorite teacher in high school, the one who had encouraged her to pursue the sciences. She'd always thought his last name would make a great first name.

"How about Caledonia for a girl? We could call her Callie."

Polly couldn't read John's face on this one. Was he kidding or...? Actually, Callie wasn't such a bad name. "Sweet. I like it."

"You do?" His brows tented together. "It was my grandmother's name." He tugged his earlobe then drank the last of his after-dinner coffee and leaned back in his chair. The night air and hint of jasmine helped engrave this more-than-fine moment in her mind. Because she didn't own a camera, she'd have to take a mental picture to remember for the rest of her life. Had she ever dreamed about casually tossing baby names around with a man before?

He'd also been by her side for the day's exciting test. Not because he'd made the appointment but because he'd wanted to be. They'd seen their baby together for the first time and celebrated with this romantic yet playful dinner by the Central Park Lake.

"I guess I'm a traditionalist at heart," he said, with that adorable half-lifted smile.

At that moment affection and something more flooded her heart for John, almost making it hard to breathe. She wanted this. So. Much.

"Why are you looking at me all funny like that?" he asked.

"I'm not looking at you funny."

"Yes you are. It's sort of like this." He imitated a goofy I'm-in-love-with-a-dove look and she burst out laughing.

"I've never made a look like that in my life!" She feigned offense.

He repeated the silly expression and they laughed together while he paid the bill and continued all the way out of the restaurant to the car.

Arriving back at his apartment, they strolled toward the doorman, holding hands. Marco greeted them with a broad and telling grin.

"Beautiful night," Marco said.

"It is," John said, lightly squeezing her hand.

All afternoon and into the evening Polly had thought she'd fallen through the looking glass into a parallel world filled with bright colors, good will, and dreams come true. John was by her side. He wouldn't desert her over the pregnancy, as she'd feared. He'd promised and she believed him.

Marco opened the door and Polly snuggled into John's shoulder as they got into the elevator, feeling like half of a real couple. The fact he'd called her dumpling earlier hadn't escaped her. He smiled down at her and brushed his fingertips across her cheek. She saw the look, the same one he'd let slip several times during dinner. He wanted her. Badly.

As he unlocked the apartment door, the only question left on Polly's mind was who would make the first move.

Before he switched on the lights he stopped her by the front door, brought his lips down to hers and kissed her tenderly. She'd missed kissing him and savored his smooth, soft lips surrounded by end-of-day stubble. He broke free from the kiss first and flipped the light switch. Under the entryway light, he cupped her face in his palms and looked deeply into her eyes with his hazel stare. She couldn't help but notice the tiny gold flecks around the pupils. They were kind eyes, and right now expressed desire. For her.

"Things will be different this time. I promise," he said.

She went up on tiptoe to reach his lips. "I liked it last time just fine." He enfolded her in his strong arms and kissed her thoroughly. She'd never felt sexier or safer in her life.

Once he'd kissed her into a mindless state where all senses vibrated on alert, he took her hand and led her down the hall, bypassing her room and heading straight for his bedroom.

She'd peeked into both his office and bedroom several times over the last week, but had never stepped inside either room. Never considered being in his bedroom again before now. It was a strongly masculine room, like him, with big, dark wood furniture and deep blue covers over the king-sized bed. The walls were pale gray and peaceful. Though peace was the last thought on her mind at the moment.

Her breathing quickened as he stepped toward her, removing her shoulder bag and unbuttoning her top. She'd brought a change of clothes to work, knowing they had a doctor's appointment and not wanting to wear work scrubs there. She started to help him with her blouse.

He stilled her hands. "Let me." Always in charge.

The thought of letting him have his way with her sent a second wave of heat across her skin and a subtle coiling in her core. She knew what letting go with John in control meant. As he unbuttoned more, the tiny raised bumps didn't go unnoticed by him, and one corner of his mouth lifted in appreciation as he delicately traced his fingertips across her clavicle. That set her nerve endings to humming all the way down to her waist.

With her top opened, he pushed it over her shoulders and kissed the side of her neck. The single kiss sprinkled more tingles across her chest, this time dipping down to her center. With nipples tight and tender, she couldn't wait for him to remove the bra she could barely squeeze into any more. He did.

One raised brow signaled he'd noticed the change in size, too. He took the weight of her breasts into his hands, gently lifting and massaging then kissing each one.

How much more could she take standing up?

He must have read her mind because he bent over and scooped her up behind the knees, carrying her to his huge bed. He pulled back the covers and lowered her then undid his buckle and removed his belt. She took the cue to take off her slacks.

"Uh-uh," he said, stopping her in mid-zip. "Let me do it."

He crawled over her on the bed, kissed her breasts again, taking longer this time, making her gasp with pleasure, then unzipped and peeled back her pants. He quickly unbuttoned his shirt and removed it then his undershirt, all the while looking at her with hungry eyes. Heat engulfed every surface of her skin in anticipation of what would follow.

She loved the sight of his body, thick muscles and broad shoulders, a wide patch of brown hair across his chest. Not the kind of man you'd see in a model's magazine but a man's man, solid, all testosterone and heat. Boy, could she feel the heat.

First taking a full and firm feel of one hip and cheek, he removed her French-cut underwear in record time. The man broke bones and realigned them for a living, his grip didn't go unnoticed. She glanced into his eyes and could tell that even now he was practicing restraint. In the next second his slacks were gone along with his briefs, and seeing him completely naked she remembered how he'd brought her to climax over and over their first night together.

She reached for his arousal but he intercepted her hand, giving her a firm look. He was taking control. Again. Fine by her. If he wanted to devour her, she'd let him.

As he dropped kisses across her chest and stomach, she arched and writhed in order to keep her hands to herself. When he reached the top of her thigh, gliding his tongue towards her center, she couldn't help herself and grasped his head, holding on for dear life as he kissed and licked her most sensitive parts. Unrelenting, he continued, and shivers rained across her flesh, exquisite sensations folding deep inside her, until she gasped and clenched her muscles uncontrollably, the release strong enough to make her buck against his mouth. He didn't let up, staying with her until she'd ridden the mind-blowing waves to the very end.

He came up smiling as she crossed her arms over her eyes and let out a long breath. "I won't survive if you keep that up."

"I'm a doctor, I know how to resuscitate." He scooped her up and began to roll onto his back, planting both hands firmly on her hips. She rolled with him, reaching for his face, kissing him, tasting herself on his lips. That deep hip and bottom massage continued seeding her desire as she lay on top of him, and she could feel his firm length beneath her belly. Before she knew it he'd hoisted her hip up and over his erection with one hand, guiding himself inside with the other. She straddled him as he slid along every sensitive spot she owned all the way inside.

"No need for a condom this time," he said, as he began to move inside her. Their gazes met and melded together in understanding.

She adjusted her hips so they fit closer together. As if it were possible, the early pregnancy made her even more sensitive to his touch, and she wondered if he felt the change, too. His powerful hips thrust upward, the strength of his thighs lifting her off the bed. She balanced herself by placing her hands on his chest, leaning into him for added pleasure. His hands cupped and squeezed her hips and soon the lazy lifts and rolls weren't enough and they turned to rocking. Faster. Firmer. Desperately penetrating.

He stopped abruptly, and in one quick move flipped her onto her back so he could drive deeper and faster yet. Jets of pleasure rocked through her with each surge. She was gone before he'd barely gotten started, the powerful grip of her muscles sending shockwaves to every part of her body. "Johnny!"

Dissolving into his determined rhythm, she wrapped her legs around his hips, urging him deeper, encouraging his release. Bucking together for several more minutes, he reawakened her need. His strength built fiercely inside as he slid in and out at a frantic pace, until he groaned and she gasped and he erupted with a growl, sharing the bliss with her one more time.

CHAPTER EIGHT

POLLY AND JOHN lay folded together in bed for several minutes. He kissed her forehead and lightly rubbed her back while he rested his eyes. She snuggled into his chest, cushioning her head on his well-padded, muscular shoulder, enjoying the thump-thump-thump of his heart.

"From now on you sleep here with me." He didn't ask, just stated how it would be.

He'd tugged his earlobe when he'd said it, the gesture she'd come to recognize whenever he spoke from his heart. Whenever he spoke the truth.

"I'd like that," she said, embracing the magnitude of his statement. Maybe it was the ultrasound, seeing their baby together, but Polly had felt the change in John tonight. He'd let down that wall between them and finally invited her inside.

He rolled her onto his chest and had a good look at her as if for the first time, playing with her chaotic hair, brushing it out of her face and hooking it behind her ears. "I can't get enough of you, Polly." His hands drifted downwards and he cupped her bottom. "It's like I've been dead and now that you woke me up, all I want is you."

With her heart swooning over this man who wanted

to be with her, wanted her to live with him, to sleep with him, to have their baby, she kissed him long and heartfelt. Afterwards their gazes met and held—his as dreamy as she knew hers must be. Was this love? Her legs came together over his, and she discovered he was a man of his word, he really couldn't get enough of her. She cuddled his building erection with the insides of her thighs, and soon he'd slipped into her again. They stared at each other as their easily coaxed passion mounted slowly but steadily.

"I've been waiting for you a long time," he said, his voice husky with desire.

"I never knew I could be so lucky," she said, wanting nothing more than to please him for the rest of her life.

After making love again, just before they finally settled down for the night John popped out of bed and padded down the hall to the kitchen. He came right back with half a dozen saltine crackers and a glass of lemon water, placing them on Polly's bedside table.

"How thoughtful," she said, tiny prickles of contentment breaking over her. "Thank you." The small gesture meant the world to her. No one since her mother had shown they cared by doing little things. He made her lunch each day, fixed dinner more often than she did, and always asked if she'd taken her prenatal vitamins and folic acid. It might not seem like a lot, but to her his thoughtfulness was everything.

"I've got to look out for you and our baby," he said, cuddling next to her, tucking the covers around them.

Polly drifted off to sleep that night grinning, happier than she could ever remember and thinking she knew for sure who the true people-pleaser was of the two of them.

* * *

The surgery on Eric Caldera had been long and difficult, but after four hours John was satisfied he'd repaired everything to the best of his ability. Twice the anesthesiologist warned that the vital signs, especially the heart rate, had increased and a small dose of beta blocker had fixed it. Eric had been watched closely after extubation to make sure all was well. Once it was established he was breathing on his own and his vitals were stable, they sent him to the recovery room.

John left the OR and yanked off his mask, leaving patient recovery to his nurses. His first order of business was to call the father in one waiting room and the mother in another. With everything having been carefully planned by social services prior to the operation, Eric's parents had agreed to wait in separate locations. That afternoon, he'd inform each of them that surgery had been a success. Their boy would be back playing whatever sport he wanted after several months of recovery and physical therapy. The mother would be first at Eric's bedside when he returned to his room and, though unhappy about playing second fiddle, the estranged father agreed to wait an extra hour before seeing his son.

Polly took report for Eric Caldera from the recovery-room nurse. "Vital signs are stable. No sign of bleeding. Unremarkable recovery."

Polly first jotted down her notes then awaited the arrival of her patient by tending to two little girls in a double room.

"I want Dr. Griffin to make me a monkey next time." The little one with red hair held her bright pink balloon princess crown from yesterday and smiled.

"I want a monkey," the second girl said. Both her

legs were in casts, one suspended above the bed in a sling. Polly noticed John had already signed both casts and added a goofy-looking happy face next to each signature.

"Dr. Griffin will be glad to make whatever kind of balloon figure you want, as long as you both take your medicine, okay?" She wasn't above making a good bargain, especially with some of the sour-tasting pills having been an issue for these two girls over the last couple of days.

"Okay," they replied in unison sing-song fashion. Sweet, it worked!

Darren stuck his head in the room. "Your post-op just arrived."

"Thanks, Dare. Could you ask Raphael to let his mother know?" With that Polly said goodbye to the girls and trotted over to Eric's room.

Still completely out of it, Eric merely moaned when Polly, Darren and the transportation clerk slid him from the gurney to the bed she'd prepared for him. In the middle of her initial assessment Eric's mother entered the room with a huge bouquet of flowers accentuated with half a dozen bright balloons.

"How's my baby doing?" Mrs. Caldera had either used extra body splash today or the star jasmine in the bouquet was emitting a particularly strong scent.

Mostly asleep, but responsive to touch, Eric crinkled up his nose as if he didn't care for the smell. His blood pressure and pulse were low, but that was to be expected with a sedated patient, and Polly remembered the recovery nurse mentioning something about beta blockers having been given to lower his heart rate during surgery. Placing the oxygen monitor on his finger, she waited for a reading.

"He seems to be doing fine." The news smoothed the deep crease between Mrs. Caldera's brows. The oxygen saturation was at the low end of normal but holding. Polly put a nasal cannula in his nostrils and turned on the wall oxygen at two liters.

After making sure Eric was comfortable, that the site of the surgery wasn't oozing blood, the IV was intact and flowing, and checking there was good circulation to his toes, she headed out to input his medication orders into the computer. On her way she spotted John heading her way, still in OR garb, looking downright sexy and authoritative. Working to control her reaction, she grinned at him then waved.

With the blue OR cap still on his head, he gave her the smile that crinkled the corners of his dark eyes, and never failed to send her heart beating double time. Also on a mission, he headed for Eric's room.

Polly set out for the medicine room to get afternoon meds for the two little girls in her other assigned room. Now that she'd bargained with them, she expected them to co-operate. In the middle of her getting the medicine, another nurse entered and she got into a conversation about a memo going around regarding blood-sugar testing and new finger-stick protocol. When the conversation ended and she'd finished pouring her meds, she heard a code blue over the loudspeaker.

"Code blue. Room 614. code blue. Room 614."

Eric's room! She rushed back to the ward only to find a crowd gathered around the door of her patient. What could have gone wrong in the few minutes she'd been away? Peering inside, she saw John was at the helm of the code in progress, calling out orders while working to re-intubate the teen. The ambu bag was in readiness in the nearby respiratory therapist's hands.

One of the medical aides assisted the mother out of the room. The woman was crying and visibly shaken. "One minute he was fine, the next he stopped breathing. What happened to my baby?"

Knowing the code team was there in full force, Polly rushed to Mrs. Caldera's side to offer support. "He's in good hands. If he's having trouble breathing, they'll fix him right up. Has your son ever been diagnosed with asthma?"

"No. When he was a baby one doctor said he had twitchy lungs, but he's never had a problem."

Could the boy have asthma and not know it? Could the sharp scent of those flowers have set him off? Or perhaps the latex in the balloons? She searched her memory for "latex allergy" on his chart, but was positive she hadn't seen any allergies noted. Latex was such a common allergy these days that John's balloons were all latex free, and the hospital had been a latex-free zone from the beginning, but who knew about florist displays? Polly was surprised Mrs. Caldera had gotten that bouquet past the hospital entrance.

Oh, God, Eric had been given a beta blocker in surgery for his elevated vital signs, if he was having an asthma attack that drug would make the effect much worse and would block the antidote. She knew John was well aware of all the medications given during the surgery, and the code team was top-notch, so she settled for worrying her lower lip with her teeth along with Mrs. Caldera.

Five minutes. She held the mother's hand and promised all would be well. Ten minutes. The rush and chaos inside the room continued in a tunnel of noise.

"We need more epi," a resident hollered from the doorway.

Leaving Mrs. Caldera with the medical aide, Polly shot across the ward to the med room to retrieve more medicine, wondering who'd been assigned to restock the crash cart that day. How could they run out of epi during a respiratory arrest? If they *had* gone through that much epi, it couldn't bode well for poor Eric.

With shaky hands Polly got the medicine and rushed to the entrance of Eric's room.

"All clear," John called out, holding the defibrillator paddles in place on the boy's chest and torso. He zapped Eric with enough joules to start a horse's heart. All eyes went to the heart monitor. No change. Flat line.

Polly delivered the epinephrine and went back to Mrs. Caldera, positioned close enough for Polly to peer through the door. They defibrillated Eric again with the same outcome.

The mood in the patient room had changed drastically. John stood sullenly at the head of the bed, head down, staring at his patient with deep remorse in his eyes. No matter that the respiratory therapist squeezed the ambu bag to force breathing, the flat-lined bedside monitor squawking its continual alarm told the full story. A young teenager had had a respiratory arrest, which had led to a full code, and he had died after surgery.

Never could anyone have foretold this outcome for a routine surgery on an otherwise healthy child, yet sometimes it happened. Truth was, surgeries were never routine.

With terror in her eyes Eric's mother sensed the change. "My baby. Is it all over? Is my baby all right?" She tore away from Polly and the medical aide and lurched for the hospital room.

Polly intercepted her but the mother's weight pushed

her off balance. Polly stood firm, held her in a hug. "Give us a second, Mrs. Caldera. Please."

In a desperate move the mother broke away. "I want to see my boy."

John stepped into the hallway just as she reached the threshold. He braced her by both shoulders, a grief-stricken look in his eyes. "I'm so sorry, Mrs. Caldera. He stopped breathing then his heart stopped. We did everything in our power to save him."

Her scream reverberated off the ward walls.

John held her tight and let her cry. He glanced over her shoulder at Polly with a grim expression. "Go and find the father in OR waiting room two and let him know what's happened. I'll explain everything to him when he gets here."

Dreading having to face a parent and tell them their child had just died, something she'd never had to do before and which wasn't normally an RN's job, she bit her lower lip and nodded solemnly, wanting some way, somehow to help John through this tragedy. Oh, God, what would she say to the father? How would she tell him the boy had been alive one minute and dead the next?

Rather than wait for the elevator, she hustled down the stairs, her legs shaky from the adrenaline pouring throughout her system. Arriving on the third floor, thinking her heart might just jump right out of her chest, she found waiting room number two. A tall, overweight, swarthy-looking man in a business suit paced the floor. The instant she arrived he looked up. "Are you Eric's nurse? Can I see him now?"

Her heart practically burst. How was she supposed to tell him? "There's been a problem, Mr. Caldera. Dr. Griffin will explain everything to you—"

He stopped in his tracks. "What do you mean there's been a problem?"

"Eric stopped breathing and—"

He grabbed her by both arms and squeezed to the point of pain. "You'd better not be telling me what I think…"

"I'm so sorry, Mr. Cal—"

He shoved her aside, exiting the room, and she bumped against the doorframe.

Rubbing her elbow, focused solely on her task, she followed him down the hall. "Mr. Caldera, it will be quicker if you take the stairs. Follow me."

With fury in his eyes, his jaw set, he came at her. She opened the door to the stairwell and he followed her inside. "It's three flights up," she said, stepping back for him to go first, "but much faster than the elevator."

"You killed him. You killed my son!" He glanced up the stairwell. "Are you trying to kill me, too?" Three steps above her, with a contorted, out-of-control, grief-stricken expression on his face, he kicked out at her, the leather sole of his shoe landing solidly on her solar plexus. It knocked the wind from her lungs and sent her hurtling down the lower flight of stairs.

Head over heels she tumbled, arms flailing, searching for purchase, enduring sharp pangs of pain as first her shoulder, then her head, then her back and bottom hit cement, all the way to the lower landing.

She couldn't breathe and clutched at the point of greatest pain, her stomach, as Eric's father raced out of the stairwell. If she could inhale she'd call for help, and warn John what was coming his way.

Trying her hardest to get to her feet, still unable to catch her breath, the dim stairway light faded to black.

* * *

Polly worked to open her eyes. Everything hurt. She wasn't at the bottom of the stairs. No, she was on a thin mattress. Cracking one eye open, the bright lights of the emergency department had her immediately snapping it shut. But not before she saw John, and felt the warmth of his hand over hers.

"How are you feeling, dumpling?" he asked, obvious concern in his voice.

"Like I got kicked down a flight of stairs."

"God, I'm so, so sorry." He leaned close, held her hand between both of his, lifting it to his mouth where he kissed her fingers. "Forgive me."

"I'll be okay." She tried an achy smile, which quickly turned into a grimace. She did a quick test—her arms moved, her ankles rotated, her knees bent, her neck twisted just fine. Of course it hurt like heck to do any of the movements, but she could move. That was a start. "I'll get over all these bangs and bruises in no time."

The rows of lines in his forehead and wary dark gaze told a different story. "I shouldn't have sent you to do my job," he said.

"John, you had your hands full with the mother. You'd just coded your patient. If the parents could get along they would have been there together. You can't do everything."

He shook his head, biting his lower lip. "I should have sent the resident to tell Mr. Caldera."

"You were in shock from the failed resuscitation. Your resident was busy with the clean-up." She reached up to hold him, and his desperate need to hold her tight warned something more was at stake. "I'm okay, I swear. I'm okay, John."

He pulled back, shaking his head. *She wasn't okay?*

The only thing she saw in his eyes was pain. "You're bleeding, sweetheart. The baby…" His voice cracked on the word. He shook his head again.

Her pregnancy was in jeopardy? Little Callie? "Did I miscarry?" Her eyes welled up as she said the word.

He shook his head—a world of weariness in his gaze. "No. They're keeping you for observation for now." One tear slid down the outer part of his left eye, soon followed by another on the right. "I'm so sorry."

She believed with all of her heart that he was sorry. But she was bleeding. Her hands covered her face as the deep emptiness of possibly losing her pregnancy took hold. Soon her hands were covered in tears as she rocked forward and back, unleashing the dammed-up tears of a lifetime filled with disappointment.

John held her and moaned. She used his shoulder to brace her forehead as she bawled until there was nothing left. The brightest spot in her life, her pregnancy, was in jeopardy.

CHAPTER NINE

IN THE CRAMPED and drab ER cubicle, John held Polly until she was ready to let go. Until she'd digested the awful news. She'd had the life nearly kicked out of her womb, and he'd been responsible for sending her to do his job. She could have been killed falling down those stairs.

The words "guilt" and "anger" didn't come close to how he judged himself.

"Can you help me to the bathroom?" she said.

"Of course." He hopped to her side and dragged the IV machine along with them. She felt so vulnerable under his care that it made his heart wrench. Against all odds he hoped this pregnancy would survive. They'd have a new start, get their chance to be parents. Hell, he'd even marry her before the baby was born. Yeah, that's what he'd do.

Would the Big Guy hear his prayer and promise?

If our baby survives, to make things up to Polly, I'll marry her and be the best damn father on the planet. If only you'll let our baby make it. Not for me, for her. No. That's a lie. For me, too. I want this. I really do.

Helping Polly into the bathroom, he closed the door and waited outside.

Soon her moan carried through the thin wall loud and clear.

"What's wrong, sweetheart?" He rushed inside to find her sitting on the toilet, dejected and bereft. "Are you okay?"

"I just miscarried." She whimpered the phrase so softly he didn't understand what she'd meant at first. As the words sank in, he dropped to his knees in front of her and put his forehead to hers. Was this some cruel joke? How many times was he supposed to lose everything dear to him? He ground his molars.

"Oh, baby, I'm so sorry. So, so sorry." Rather than call for the nurse, he helped clean her up and walked her back to the bed. He put on the call light for the nurse, then made Polly comfortable, but there was no way on earth anything he could do would take away her loss or her pain. She'd lost the baby. Their baby. Her tears ran without effort down her cheeks. So did his as sorrow wrapped around his chest and squeezed the last of his feelings from him.

When the nurse arrived he told her what had happened.

"We'll need to schedule a D&C," he said, knowing the routine protocol for such things.

"I'll get right on that, Doctor," the nurse said on the way out the door.

John held Polly's fragile body until she fell asleep. Pacing the tiny ER cubicle, thoughts stabbed at his conscience. He hadn't been able to protect his wife and future child before, and look at him now—he'd sent Polly into the eye of the storm. He hadn't been there for Lisa and now he hadn't been there when Polly had needed him most. Hell, it was his job to tell parents when their children died, yet distracted by the failed code, in partial denial, and concentrating on Mrs. Caldara he'd taken the easy way out and sent Polly to fetch the father.

She could have been killed! Now she'd lost her baby.

What kind of man was he?

A man who didn't deserve to be loved by Polly or anyone else on earth.

Her lids fluttered and cracked open. He sat straighter. "You need anything?"

She studied him for several seconds with reflective eyes, as if she could read his thoughts, then shook her head soberly and went back to napping. He reached for her hand out of obligation, his fingers nearly as numb as his heart had become over the last few hours, and he stayed by her side for the remainder of the afternoon. In limbo. Lost, without a tether. Prayers unanswered. His heart cracked apart. He had nothing left to offer.

"They're ready for her in the procedure room," the nurse said at the cubicle entrance.

John jumped to his feet, prepared to go along with Polly.

As if she'd sensed his rote response, she looked at him. "I'll be fine. You don't have to come along."

"Are you sure?" He didn't even put up a fight.

"Positive." She squeezed his dull grip and he kissed her forehead, though his lips were numb, too.

"See you later, then," he said, watching the gurney roll down the corridor, not sure he recognized his own flat and distant voice.

Polly put her stained work clothes in the plastic bag provided by the hospital. She'd changed into the clothes John had brought from home. "I'm ready," she said that evening.

"Okay." He stood, his eyes drifting everywhere but

to hers. "I'll bring the car round and meet you at the ER entrance."

The transportation clerk waited nearby with a wheelchair. Protocol was protocol, and Polly felt too weak and achy to fight it.

When she met him at the curbside of the hospital exit, John hopped out of the car ready to assist her from the wheelchair, seeming robotic and acting out of duty. Yet he was here, she reminded herself, attempting to hold onto the positive. At least he hadn't run away from their depressing mess.

His hand felt chilly to the touch when he helped her stand. Again, his eyes avoided hers and she curled her lower lip and chewed on it just to have something else to concentrate on.

Unable to think of a single thing to say, Polly remained quiet on the drive on Central Park South toward Sutton Place, choosing instead to watch the tree-lined streets they passed. Once they were back in the apartment, he helped her to the guest room, where he'd already pulled back the covers in readiness. He must have planned making the change from lover to guest when he'd come back earlier to get her change of clothes and the car.

"I thought you'd be more comfortable in here," he said when she'd sent him a questioning glance. The ball of emotion swelling in her chest sank to her stomach when she noticed how detached he seemed. Cold even.

Too weak and bumped up to protest, she got under the covers and let him tuck her in.

Every considerate thing he did felt distant and done out of obligation as the evening wore on. He brought her a tray with soup and crackers, helped her to the bathroom when she wanted to get ready to turn in for the night, and assisted her back to bed as if she were a fragile ninety-year-old woman. Making her feel nothing like the woman he'd made love to.

Polly had hoped to curl into his protective embrace tonight. To sleep next to him and feel his heat radiate over her, healing her. Together they could get through this by clinging close and comforting one another. She'd hoped to regain the strength that had hemorrhaged out during the course of this incredibly long day by being by his side. But John had sent her back to the guest room without even asking her, as if without the pregnancy he no longer had reason to make her a part of his life.

What they'd made together was no more.

She was plumb out of tears as she lay in the darkness, staring at the white ceiling.

Today she'd been kicked down the stairs, she'd lost her baby, and somehow during the horrific series of events she may as well have been kicked in the gut again, because now she'd lost John, too.

Three days later Polly insisted on going back to work. She couldn't bear the thought of being a prisoner in John's apartment another day, and longed for the distraction of a busy orthopedic ward. They'd hardly spoken since the miscarriage and she felt more like an obligation than a lover and a grieving partner.

At times he'd pulled so deeply inside himself that she'd felt like an invasive war lord, demanding attention whenever she'd tried to engage him in the simplest things.

"Want to help make a salad?" she'd said the previous night, insisting making her own dinner.

"You go ahead," he said. "I'm not hungry."

She ate alone while he sequestered himself in his

study. They hadn't taken one meal together since the miscarriage.

At work, word traveled fast. During the Monday morning report Polly accepted each and every hug from her friends and fellow staff. It felt good to be back. At least in Darren's and Brooke's eyes she saw genuine sadness, something missing from John's. When she looked into his eyes, the unfathomable detachment made it seem like he wasn't there. As if he'd checked out for good.

Piling the pain of losing John on top of the heartache of her miscarriage, she could barely stand up straight. The house had become heavy with silence, washed in colorless depression. At night she'd hole up in her room working on a bitter-sweet but necessary project.

Warm hands rested on her shoulders. For an instant Polly imagined John had walked up behind her. He'd barely touched her since she'd lost the baby. Maybe there was still hope? Maybe all could be well again? She turned to find Raphael, his kind eyes probing hers, and she tried not to look disappointed. "You've got a phone call," he said.

"Oh, thanks." Shaken out of her thoughts, she forced a shift in her attitude. She was at work and needed to give it her full concentration. She punched the blinking light and picked up the receiver. "This is Polly."

"Ms. Seymour, it's Mrs. Goldman." Her landlady. "I have someone interested in taking your room. I know you paid me for an extra month, but…"

"No. Please, Mrs. Goldman, I'd like to keep that room a little while longer. I'm paid up through August and September. If you'd like, I'll pay for October now, too."

Agreeing on a compromise, Polly hung up the phone

feeling less helpless in her current living situation by having another option.

"Who in the blazes messed with the bed traction in Room Twelve?" John sounded like an ornery bear as he headed toward Brooke at the nurses' station. His rugged, masculine appeal had vanished along with his civil mood.

"P.T. was in there earlier," Brooke said, straightening her shoulders and making her taller-than-average frame seem even taller.

"Get them up here, now!" he growled, and stormed off to the next room.

Brooke glanced at Polly, alarm in her eyes. How quickly they'd forgotten how difficult John could be. No longer an avowed people-pleaser, Polly shrugged, realizing she'd also lost her magic touch where John was concerned, and went seeking solace in her assigned patient room. A teeny-bopper with bright eyes and a lively attitude was just the distraction she needed. *Sweet.* And thank heavens for small favors.

"Who forgot to put Brandon Seamus in the CPM machine today?" John's baritone carried all the way across the ward.

Darren popped his head up as Brandon was his patient. "Last week we had an in-service from P.T. that said the continuous passive motion device didn't make a difference by six weeks post-surgery."

"Did I DC the order?"

"No, sir."

"Then get off your duff and put his knee in the machine. Now!"

Polly came out of her patient room, shaken and embarrassed for John. "There's no reason to speak to Darren like that. He was following the recommendation of Physical Therapy."

"Did I ask your opinion?"

"I don't care if you asked it or not. You don't have the right to talk to your staff like that."

He looked at her as if he hated her and everyone else in the world, harrumphed and walked away. "I'll have a little talk with P.T. about going over my head and disregarding my orders," he said when he passed Brooke.

Knowing deep in her heart the pros and cons of using a CPM machine after knee procedures wasn't the issue, Polly felt queasy for John. She wished she could find a way to reach him before he quarantined himself completely from the world of the living.

That evening John cooked again. Maybe it was his way of apologizing? After having a well-prepared but tasteless meal in silence, Polly finished putting the dishes in the dishwasher. "I think I'll go for a walk to the park." There were two parks nearby and the one she had in mind overlooked the East River.

"I'll go with you."

She'd known he'd say that. Not because he wanted to be with her but because he wanted to protect her. From what? She'd walk to a beautiful park in a well-to-do neighborhood. It was still only early August, and it wasn't even dark out yet. But she'd depended on his twisted sense of obligation to accompany her, to open up the opportunity to talk. Maybe, while they walked and enjoyed the evening, she could crack that ever-hardening shell he was doing such a fine job of constructing.

The night air was still thick and humid. Polly chose a brisk pace and John had no problem keeping up. If anything, she had to widen her stride to match his.

"So, what's been going on?" she asked.

"What do you mean?" He gave her a look as if she'd just landed from planet crazy.

"You've been very bristly."

"I've bent over backwards to give you space, to help you heal."

Silence doesn't heal anything. She didn't want to go there right now. She wanted to intervene on her co-workers' behalf, before John drove them to resign one by one by one. The orthopedic kids didn't need to deal with constant staff turnover along with all their other ailments.

"I'm talking about work, about how you're chewing everyone's heads off, like before I came..." Her voice drifted off. She didn't want to suggest she'd had anything to do with his turnaround in attitude at work... before everything had gone to hell in a handbasket.

"Nurses are tough. They can take me. Always have."

End of subject.

They entered the park lined with red bricks and bushes. She found an empty bench facing the river and sat. Inhaling, she realized the air was nothing like the sea. This humongous East River by the huge city smelled like life itself—of car exhausts, hot cement, hordes of people—yet the pewter-colored water overcame it all and offered a hint of refreshment. Polly needed to be refreshed. Living on this side of town with John, however briefly, this view had become one of her favorites in the city.

A jogger passed by. A hundred yards behind a woman with a stroller walked her baby. Polly had to look away, choosing to focus on the long steel sculpture of the Queensboro Bridge rather than lost possibilities.

"People can take all kinds of things, but they shouldn't have to. Your berating everyone wears skin thin." She reached for his hand, a gesture she'd given up on since he'd brought her home from the hospital. "You're hurting, John, and you're taking it out on the people around you."

It wasn't obvious, but she felt his hand recoil the tiniest bit. "Look, you handle things your way, and I'll handle them mine." She let go of his hand just as the woman with the stroller came by.

They sat for several more minutes staring at the river, thousands of necessary words going unspoken. How could she get through to John in his emotionally shutdown state, where the only feeling allowed to appear was anger?

"You ready to go back?" he said. "I've got an early surgery tomorrow."

With that, they walked back to his apartment in silence, Polly feeling as though she had cement bricks chained to her ankles.

By the end of the second day back at work and after several more outbursts from John towards the staff, Polly dreaded going home with him again. How much could she take of his foul mood while she grieved? And yet at home he'd become docile, so docile, in fact, she'd begun to suspect he was no longer alive.

"I think I'll walk home," she said, at his office door that Tuesday evening.

He stood and came around his desk. For the first time in days she saw an expression besides anger on his face, but she couldn't make out exactly what it meant. "But you're too weak to walk all the way home." With brows lowered, looking gruff, his words didn't match.

"I managed working all day yesterday and today without problems. I'll be fine."

"Only two days back at work, five since the miscarriage. All the more reason to let me drive you."

Obligation. Pure obligation. Though it was the first time he'd mentioned her miscarriage since the day it'd happened, and that struck Polly as progress. But not enough to want to spend another painful night in his presence, longing to crack his hardened shell, to get back to that wonderful man she'd known so briefly. John wouldn't allow it.

"So we'll have more time to sit in that dead apartment of yours and stare at each other?"

His brows shot up. Surprise tinted his brown stare. "I thought you'd appreciate some peace and quiet."

"More like rest in peace, you mean? Just bury me and get it over with, why don't you?"

He folded his arms. "I've done everything I possibly can to make you comfortable."

"Including shutting me out."

"I didn't think we needed to talk about our loss just yet."

"You banished me from your room, John."

With the topic becoming personal, he strode around her and closed his office door. "You can't stand the sight of me."

"What in heaven's name gave you that impression?"

"It's my fault you lost the baby. Why would you want to be anywhere near me, let alone sleep in the same bed?"

She shook her head. "You don't know me at all, do you?" With that, she swung open the door. Didn't the man know the meaning of comfort, both giving and getting, by sharing sadness? "I'll be home later, don't wait up," she said, and took off down the hall determined to find something to do to keep her busy until it was time to go to bed. Maybe she'd stop at the bookstore the next block over and read until she couldn't keep her eyes open. Oh, wait, there was that letter she needed to write, she shouldn't put it off another day. She could write the letter at the bookstore.

Anything not to have to face the man who'd checked out on her when she'd needed him most.

CHAPTER TEN

TWO MORE DAYS of living with John had drained the flow of energy from Polly's core. She could barely lift her head off the pillow. Would this be the story of her life? Drifting from person to person, never really cared for, ever to be seen as an obligation and nothing more?

She sat bolt upright. No. She wouldn't settle for that. She deserved more. She was young, she could get pregnant again if she ever found the right man. Melancholy thoughts about what she'd almost had with John, how he could be "the right man", how her dreams of having her own family had been just within reach but had been snatched away at the last moment invaded her thinking. A cruel joke.

Getting out of bed, she grabbed her robe and headed for the shower. Passing the kitchen, she smelled fresh coffee brewing, piquing her senses. Now that she could drink coffee again, she'd pour herself a cup and enjoy it. She was damned if she intended to live the rest of her life like a ghost, the way John had chosen to do. In his case, an angry, bitter ghost.

She got into the shower and scrubbed herself to near shining, ready to take on the world again. But this time she wasn't going to fall back into her old ways. Nope. From now on the only person she intended to please was herself. This would be the summer and fall of Polly, and she wouldn't let an out-of-touch-with-his-own-feelings sad-sack like John drag her down one more inch.

As she toweled off and combed out her hair, she made plans. She'd ask Darren to help her move out over the weekend and she'd go back to Mrs. Goldman's and put this sad episode of her life behind her. Little Caledonia would forever have a special place in her heart, and she'd honor her miscarried baby by living each day, not merely existing as John had chosen to do. She couldn't be around negative people any more. She just couldn't.

The John she had glimpsed and fallen in love with was long gone. How could she possibly tie herself to a man who wasn't even able to tell her how sad he was after the miscarriage? He'd cried half a dozen tears at the ER, but since then an iron wall had been erected, and she could waste a lifetime trying to scale it but never succeeding.

No. There was nothing here for her at the 56th Street apartment. Striding down the hall, she came to an abrupt stop when she saw John in the kitchen, eating a bowl of cereal, and was perplexed by the pop of feelings in her chest. When he saw her there was a sheepish quality to his glance. Surely he knew—how could he not?—he'd become unbearable at work and to live with. Yet what was up with that tiny circle of softening in her chest? She had to ignore it, harden up like he had, or she'd never get away.

"Good morning, John," she said, as if she'd walked into a business meeting.

"Polly." He kept spooning the cereal to his mouth yet watched her move around the kitchen.

She poured herself a cup of coffee, spilled in some

creamer, took a sip and smiled. "Hmm, I've really missed this stuff."

His lips quirked but not enough to call it a smile.

"I've decided to walk to work today."

He'd finished his cereal and dropped the bowl into the sink. "It's supposed to get really hot, you may want a ride home."

"No, thanks." She rummaged through the cupboard to find a bowl and poured herself some cereal, too. They liked the same brand, just as they liked so many other similar things.

Didn't matter. That was the past. This was her future. The new Polly only lived for Polly now, regardless of a guy's taste in cereal.

"I've got surgery in an hour, so if you're sure you don't want a ride…"

"I'm sure."

He stopped before he left the kitchen, gray suit slacks fitting perfectly, white dress shirt tucked in over a flat stomach, his muscular arms apparent through the sleeves. She didn't want to notice any of it, but couldn't help herself. He turned round and studied her, as if seeing her for the first time. Maybe he was wondering what he was doing, letting a stranger share his home. Or maybe he sensed the new, determined Polly, the one eager to take life by the horns again. She honestly couldn't tell from the gaze he gave her. Neither did she care.

"I'll try not to make any scenes at work today."

Well, that was something anyway. She cocked her head and tossed him an it's-about-time look. "Good, because that stuff gets old, fast." Then took another drink of coffee, rather than let her heart soften one tiny bit more.

He twitched a sad smile with resigned eyes, and left.

She heard the front door click closed, and she ate the rest of her cereal feeling curiously alone. It didn't matter. She wouldn't be living here much longer.

Before she left for work, she ventured down the hall to John's study, deciding to check it out just this once. At first glance it was a typical office with dark wood desk, blotter, computer and printer. Piles of medical journals covered one section.

Something on the book case against the wall caught her eye. A small glass orb sitting on a solid gold holder with the inscription "Forever", and inside the orb two wedding rings lay overlapped. Not only did Lisa live on in his heart, she lived real as life itself in his office. Polly had wondered what precious object John had kept from Lisa. It turned out he'd kept the whole marriage. His vows had gone beyond "till death do us part." Evidently they extended for ever. She had never stood a chance.

"Darren," she said later that morning at work, "is there any way you can help me move this weekend?"

"That bad, huh?" The ex-navy man may have let his body go, but his posture was always erect. He turned to look into her eyes. "Are you sure it's the right thing to do? I mean, you just moved in."

"It's a long story, Dare. I just need to get away. I don't have much stuff. All I need is one car trip to the Lower East Side, otherwise I'll have to make a dozen trips on the subway."

He put his hand on top of hers. "I'll help you. Does he know?"

"Here's the deal. I want my moving out to have some impact. If I come out and tell him, he'll just say...whatever, and I need him to feel something. Other than anger, he's forgotten how to feel."

She folded her arms and chewed her lower lip. "I probably don't mean anything to him any more, but I want him to be hit by my not being there." She shook her head, giving a brief exhalation through her nose. "He probably won't even notice I'm gone."

Darren leveled a serious look at her. "You don't see it, but I do. That guy is crazy mad in love with you. Men don't process stuff the same way women do. Maybe you should be patient."

"I've been patient all my life, Dare. I'm done. All I've ever done was tag along, grateful to have a place to live, grateful for whatever crumbs I got. I need more than that now. I deserve it."

"We all deserve things. Life doesn't always co-operate, that's all. Take Dr. Rodriguez and Dr. Woods that everyone has been talking about these last several weeks. They were supposed to be in love and some lawsuit got in the way. Here's a little surprise for you—everyone has them broken up for good, but not me. Everyone say's they've got too much to overcome and they're both too stubborn, but not me. I see how he watches her whenever they're both on our ward. She acts all 'oh, he doesn't know I exist' but he's totally aware of her.

"That's how it is with Dr. Griffin and you. Polly, the man has lost everything in his life, now you're leaving him, too. I'm your friend and I'm asking you to think about not moving out. Maybe just give it some more time."

Surprised by how observant Darren had been, she stared at him and considered his caution.

"I don't have any more time. I'm a shadow in John's

house and I need to be so much more than that. Until he snaps out of it, I may as well be a ghost." She put her hand on Darren's arm. "I can't be a ghost any more. Thank you for being my friend and helping me move."

"Sure, kid. Someone's got to look out for a small-town girl like you in the Big Apple."

She hugged him and they spent the rest of their lunch hour working out the details. Polly knew John liked to go to his athletic club on Sunday afternoons for racket-ball, and she planned to be gone by the time he got home.

On Monday morning John waited for Polly to get up, but didn't hear a thing. He'd gotten home late last night as after racketball he'd gone out to dinner with Carl, his friend since childhood, had laid the whole sorry tale at the guy's feet and had gotten some insight on what a jackass he'd been. Most importantly, Carl had given him some solid advice. This morning John put his wedding rings inside a box and packed them away in the office closet. Lisa was gone. She was never coming back. Polly was here. Alive.

Her door had been closed when he'd come home last night, and he hadn't wanted to disturb her, even though he'd had some major apologies to make and had found it hard to wait to get them off his chest. Regardless, he'd gone directly to bed.

Why did the place feel so deadly quiet this morning? The hairs on his arms rose. He knocked and jiggled the doorhandle. "Polly?"

He opened the door to an empty room. Every breath of life she'd brought into his world had dissipated. The effect of negative air sucked the wind from his lungs.

She'd left him. After the total ass he'd been lately, why should he be surprised?

Entering her room, a pang of loneliness dug so deep it may as well have taken him by the lapels and thrown him against the wall. She was gone. Had left without saying goodbye.

He walked around the room, inhaling the tell-tale scent of Polly. Lemon water and flowery bath gel, and the bouquet of her gloriously wavy hair on the pillow. God, he missed her. He'd played his hand so incompetently he didn't deserve to have her back. But how could he go on without her?

He searched the room. Circling the bed, he found the table drawer ajar. Inside, something pink caught his eye. He pulled open the drawer and discovered a pair of tiny booties. One pink. One blue.

The air went out of his lungs again as he realized the significance, as his heart squeezed with anguish. With eyes stinging, the whisper of what John had lost became reality. Their baby was gone. He'd lost another part of himself to tragedy.

How much more could he bear?

Tears tracked down his cheeks as he sat on the bed and fingered the tiny slippers, perfectly knit by Polly. How long would he punish himself for his mistakes? Something crackled inside the pink slipper and he put his index finger inside, practically filling the entire bootie, and found a small folded piece of tissue-thin paper.

Opening it, he had to squint several times to clear the burning tears blurring his vision.

Dear Caledonia (Callie) or Sterling (Mort)

Oh, God, how was he supposed to be able to read the note? His heartache deflated and oozed out onto his skin, making him fragile and achy.

Polly had written a letter to their miscarried baby. He swallowed, unsuccessfully, the knot of anguish in his throat and continued to read.

I know it's foolish to write you this letter, but I needed to tell you how happy I was when I found out you were growing inside me. I've never been so lucky in my life. For once I would have some-body to love with all of my heart, someone who would look up to me and love me back.

I remember my mother, and I know how im-portant a mother is. I miss her as much as I miss you. I'm so sorry I didn't get to know you, or to be your mommy. We would have been so happy...

Pain tore at John's throat and down his chest. He could hardly breathe it hurt so much. She'd taken the words he'd buried inside and put them on paper. He wanted to be a father more than anything, but had been afraid to admit it. He'd substituted his young patients for his lost child. How could such a young woman as Polly be so much wiser than him?

John clenched his jaws and cried silently over all he'd lost. Soon the intensity of his grief and loss over-came him. Foreign, keening sounds emitted from his throat over everything gone or dead in his life. Finally, he let it all out. He hadn't sobbed this much since 9/11.

Oh, God. But Polly was alive. He'd practically ig-nored her and now he'd let the best thing to happen to him in over a decade slip away. What a fool he was.

Polly was the most honest person he'd ever met. She'd been kicked in the gut by life yet had refused to lie down. She was optimism and energy and sweetness in the flesh. Instead of burying her feelings the way

he had, she'd put them on paper and written to her unborn child. She'd suffered terribly, losing the baby, and
when she'd needed him most, what had he done? He'd
pulled inward, sent her to the guest room, as if turning
his back on her.

How stupid could a guy get?

Maybe it was time for him to quit kicking himself.
Sure, he'd screwed up plenty, but Polly was living proof
that a life could change. He wanted to change for her.

He'd made so many mistakes—too many to count—
but he couldn't let Polly be one of them. He loved her.
Absolutely. He did. There was no doubt in his mind.
And he missed her, with all the enthusiasm and spirit
she'd brought to his dull life. He craved her, the desire
and lust she'd reawakened in him. She'd made his life
so much better on countless levels.

But more than anything, he needed her back.

She'd never felt wanted since her mother had died,
and he couldn't change that, but he sure as hell could
change her not feeling wanted by him! She deserved
to know without a doubt that she was loved, and cherished, and would be for the rest of her life if she'd just
give him a second chance.

There was only one way to get his point across. In
person. He picked up the phone, called work, spoke to
Brooke and made sure Polly was there.

He ran down the hall and splashed some water in his
face, then did everything in his power to make himself
look presentable. He wanted to look good the next time
he faced the love for the rest of his life.

Polly flushed the line in the IV piggyback after deliv-
ering the antibiotics to four-year-old Jeffrey Pomeroy
the third. The adorable little boy slept soundly even

though he was inside a body cast that defied the word "comfort".

When she'd disposed of the syringe she noticed Dr. Woods across the ward, looking at a computer. Not more than fifteen feet away stood Dr. Rodriguez, pretending to read a report, but he was watching her. How could the woman not feel that smoldering gaze? Before long, Dr. Woods's pretty blonde head lifted and her gaze drifted towards and locked with Dr. Rodriguez's dark and mesmerizing stare. Quicker than a humming-bird, her eyes flitted away, but it was undeniably there, that one intense second had said it all—they definitely weren't over by a long shot. Polly shook her head and smiled to herself. That Darren knew a lot more than he let on.

She went back into the patient room and prepared to give her second patient a bed bath. All the while she thought about Dr. Woods and Dr. Rodriguez, and the one person she couldn't get out of her head or heart, John.

"Polly Seymour?" She heard John's distinct voice echo off the walls. "Polly. Get out here!" He'd promised to behave after last Friday's outburst. Oh, God, had he lost it altogether? Would someone be calling Security and taking him away soon?

Sheepishly peeking around the threshold first, she ventured out of the patient room. Anything to quiet him down until Security could arrive. The poor patients and their families didn't need to be subjected to his unpredictable and escalating mood swings. The constant ache in her heart since she'd left him panged deeper.

Of course a crowd had assembled to watch the poor man's demise. Brooke and Rafael, Darren, not looking the least bit alarmed, and all the other nurses and technicians she'd grown to know and enjoy from working with them. Even Dr. Woods and Dr. Rodriguez were there, still exchanging quick passionate glances, while lingering on the fringes of the group, most likely wondering what was going on with their colleague. Everyone huddled around the nurses' station, watching John, who looked amazingly dashing for a man on the verge of professional suicide.

"Polly." He spoke the word now, softened the tone of his voice, as if her appearance had taken the edge off. He smiled an honest-to-God, no mistaking expression of his happiness at seeing her.

Though shaking inside, she hoped beyond hope that if she played it cool and calculated she could de-escalate his impending meltdown. Polly schooled her voice. "Yes, John?" She could humor him until the hospital security squad arrived.

"You forgot something."

She stood cemented to the spot, her heart rapping a wild rhythm all the way up to her ears, watching as he pulled out the booties from the pocket of his doctor's jacket. Heat started at her clavicles and traveled to her neck, soon invading her cheeks. He'd found them. He'd discovered she'd let herself get so carried away with loving and longing for her baby that she'd knitted booties. Booties for a baby who would never be born.

Did he think she was pitiful?

"I need you to finish these," he said. "No. That's not entirely true." His voice was now low enough for only those in the front row of the crowd to hear. Others got on tiptoe and leaned in towards the spectacle of their department chief confronting the newest staff nurse. "What I need…is you. You, Polly. The thing is, I finally realize I can't live without you."

He came toward her, took her hand, and that tender look he'd had after each time they'd made love was back in his eyes.

"I love you, Polly. You belong with me. You've got to finish these booties because we're going to need them. After you marry me and…"

Applause broke out. Time stopped. With her heart reeling, she quickly glanced around the room, catching Dr. Woods and Dr. Rodriguez smiling at each other. Beside them, Darren grinned first at the lovebird doctors then at her.

"I told you so," Darren mouthed.

Real time snapped back in, ungluing Polly from the spot, and she grabbed John by the elbow and whisked him away to the consultation room at the far end of the ward. She closed the door. What she had to say needed to be said in private.

"What makes you think I *want* to marry you?"

He wore a goofy grin and dreamy eyes, and she could tell there would be no reasoning with him. "Because you're a smart girl, and I love you, and I want you in my life." His fingertips traced the length of her jaw.

She dropped her head back and stared at the ceiling for guidance. No one had ever wanted her before, but that was no reason to let him seduce her with words.

He grasped her neck, brought her head up straight in line with his lips and delivered a tender, sincere kiss. Nothing fancy, just his warm lips to her startled ones, and she felt his touch all the way down to the tips of her toes.

"I was a total jerk after the miscarriage, but I've come to my senses." He dangled the booties before her eyes as if to hypnotize her. "You did this on purpose, didn't you? Left these behind."

She glanced at his delving, dark eyes and quickly studied a speck on his white doctor's coat. "Maybe."

He took both of her hands in his. "I know you've never really felt like you belonged anywhere, honey, but I'm the guy to end it. The buck stops with me. I'm your man. The one who loves you. I'm the man who wants to spend the rest of his life with you." He looked so deeply into her eyes she was positive he could read her brainwaves, which were dancing around erratically and happily over his proposal. "So I guess the question of the day is, do you love me?"

Tiny pins stabbed behind her eyes as tears that she'd sworn she'd never cry again for John Griffin materialized. "I couldn't bear it if you ever shut me out again, John. You have to promise me you'll always talk to me no matter how hard or how horrible your feelings are."

He held her arms and kept her steady. Steady as his warm brown gaze. "I promise to love and honor you, to share the good, the bad, and the ugly, whether you want to hear it or not." His lopsided smile appeared. "How's that for opening up?"

How could she not adore a face like that? A tiny laugh escaped her trembling lips.

"I do love you, Johnny."

His smile morphed into a huge grin and spread from jaw to jaw as he took her into his arms. "So it's settled, then." He grew serious and kissed her again, this time with much more gusto, enough to spread warmth across her chest and make her toes curl in her clogs. After several more seconds of deeply attentive kisses dazzling enough to make her head swim and her heart believe he truly wanted and loved her, he stopped.

"Then let's blow this joint and get married, dumpling. Do you like the sound of that? The married part, I mean?"

Staring into the eyes of the man she'd fallen head over heels in love with on short notice, the man she'd run the gamut of any other long-term relationship in her life, but this time on hyper-speed, she could only think of one succinct yet most appropriate answer.

"I do."

EPILOGUE

Eleven months later...

"BE CAREFUL!" JOHN SAID, jumping up to help Polly walk across the living room.

"I'm fine, Johnny, seriously." She held her swollen belly as if it might fall off her body if she didn't, and wobbled toward the kitchen.

John tagged along behind her. "How's the back?"

"Achy," she said, looking into the face of the man she loved and trusted more than anyone on earth, "but I'll survive."

"I've got your suitcase packed and ready to go, just like the midwife instructed," he said, hovering like a penguin on a newborn. "Say the word and we'll go to the hospital."

Polly put her hands on her back, the habit she'd developed during the last few months of her pregnancy, and smiled at John. "It's not quite time yet, honey-bunches, but thanks."

Once in the kitchen, she opened a cupboard and started to reach for a glass. John jumped between her and the glassware and got one down for her. "Water?"

"Yes, please."

"Sit. I'll bring it to you." He pointed toward the table and she obeyed.

Since she'd been on maternity leave for the last two weeks, with twenty-four hours a day of intense attention from John and a uterus that felt ready to explode, no one was more anxious to deliver the babies than she. Babies. Yes. Two. A boy and a girl. She pinched herself. It wasn't a dream. Polly liked to blame those pink and blue booties for the twins. Maybe if she'd stuck to one color she wouldn't feel as if she had a small crowd inside her. But with John's loving care, the four of them had been getting along beautifully over the past nine months.

If she didn't count the constant acid reflux and a diaphragm so under pressure that taking deep breaths was almost impossible, she'd say life was perfect.

Polly sat on the kitchen chair, and John was quick to pull out another so she could elevate her feet, then he handed her the water. Just as she swallowed her first sip, Callie and Sterling decided to take a run around the indoor gym and pool.

"Oh!" She quickly set the glass on the table and sat straighter.

"What is it?" John jumped to his feet again then dropped to one knee in front of her. The poor man hadn't had a moment's rest since she'd announced with pride he'd made her pregnant again. And Polly had never felt more wanted and cared for.

She couldn't talk as pain escalated like she'd never experienced before. Her eyes bugged out and she held her breath.

"Don't forget to breathe, dumpling, remember what

the birthing coach told you." John looked at his watch. These days she really did feel like a dumpling.

The labor pain began to let up and she relaxed into the chair. "How far apart are we now?"

"Four minutes. Are you ready to go to the hospital yet?"

She shook her head. "Let's walk a little bit first, okay?"

She loved her evening walks along the East River, even though it was hotter than usual this July. The last thing she wanted to do was show up at Labor and Delivery when she hadn't even begun to dilate, and a walk by the river might just be the ticket to moving her labor along. Dr. Bernstein was thrilled she'd carried the pregnancy the whole nine months, but with John's tender loving care she wasn't the least bit surprised.

John didn't look convinced that a walk during early labor was such a great idea but, as with almost everything else in their life together, he wanted to please her. "Okay, then, let's go." He helped her to her feet and they headed for the door.

By the time they'd reached the street, Polly was having another contraction. She stood perfectly still and tried to breathe. John rubbed her shoulders and lower back as she did.

"This time it was three minutes," he said. "Change your mind about going to the hospital yet?"

The contraction had lasted longer and felt more intense, and even though John was a doctor she wanted to be around the trained midwife and OB nurses when she delivered. She nodded. "Okay, call the hospital and let them know we're coming in."

John's eyes went wide as he dug out his cell phone

and pushed autodial. "It's really happening?" He squeezed her hand, excitement and fear registering in his gaze.

"Yes. Maybe you should get my suitcase."

"And leave you alone?"

"Marco can watch me until you get back."

John hesitated, but when Marco got a chair for Polly to sit on while she waited, he dashed back into the building, heading for the elevator.

Ten hours later...

John watched his wife snuggle with their newborns. Her hair had grown thicker and curlier with the pregnancy, and the sight of her holding the twins, well, she was never more beautiful. In awe, he looked on. The babies had tiny fingers and toes, and nostrils that couldn't possibly pass enough air to keep them alive. Amazing. Nothing short of a miracle.

His kids. His wife.

If he'd performed back-to-back hip replacements, he couldn't have been more exhausted, yet being with his new family energized him. Polly had worked like a trouper during labor, and he'd been by her side every step of the way. The sight of Caledonia entering the world had brought tears to his eyes and when he got to hold Sterling seconds after his birth, he'd thought he might pass out for fear of dropping or injuring his son.

What a team they'd been, Polly in mid-contraction breathing and pushing, John holding her hand, cheering her on. *You can do it. Don't give up.* Like a fearless warrior she'd gone through labor fighting her way to victory, eager to get to the prize. Now, watching his children with their mother, the abundance of love and blessings welling in his heart made his eyes go bleary. Nothing could ever match this most special moment in time.

"We did it," Polly said. "We made beautiful babies."

He cupped her face and saw his children squirm in Polly's arms. "With me as their father they only had a fifty-fifty chance of that beautiful part, you know."

She grinned and shook her head. "They'll be strong and smart because of you."

"And they'll always know they're loved."

"Yes. Just like I do."

After all the losses John had experienced in his forty years on the planet, through Polly he'd learned to trust that life could still bestow wonders and joy, too. She'd complained he was way too protective of her, but she'd slowly gotten used to it. She'd had no choice.

"Now I'll be on triple duty, watching over all of you," he said, pride ringing from each word.

"You poor man, you're bound to wear out!" She feigned worry, but he knew she was delighted he'd promised to always be there for his family.

"Never."

He snapped a picture with his phone and sent it to Brooke to share with the hospital staff.

"We're going to have to work as a team with these little dumplings," she said.

He'd been warned by younger colleagues that nothing was more difficult than being a parent.

"We'll be the perfect team," he said. "You. Me. Callie and Sterling."

John gazed at his family in the hospital bed while reeling with ever-expanding love in his heart. Since meeting and opening his life and love to Polly, becoming a husband and now a father, he knew one thing deeper and better than anything else in the world. No matter how many curve balls life threw at him, as long as Polly and the kids were by his side he would survive anything.

* * * * *

Mills & Boon® Hardback
June 2013

ROMANCE

The Sheikh's Prize	Lynne Graham
Forgiven but not Forgotten?	Abby Green
His Final Bargain	Melanie Milburne
A Throne for the Taking	Kate Walker
Diamond in the Desert	Susan Stephens
A Greek Escape	Elizabeth Power
Princess in the Iron Mask	Victoria Parker
An Invitation to Sin	Sarah Morgan
Too Close for Comfort	Heidi Rice
The Right Mr Wrong	Natalie Anderson
The Making of a Princess	Teresa Carpenter
Marriage for Her Baby	Raye Morgan
The Man Behind the Pinstripes	Melissa McClone
Falling for the Rebel Falcon	Lucy Gordon
Secrets & Saris	Shoma Narayanan
The First Crush Is the Deepest	Nina Harrington
One Night She Would Never Forget	Amy Andrews
When the Cameras Stop Rolling...	Connie Cox

MEDICAL

NYC Angels: Making the Surgeon Smile	Lynne Marshall
NYC Angels: An Explosive Reunion	Alison Roberts
The Secret in His Heart	Caroline Anderson
The ER's Newest Dad	Janice Lynn

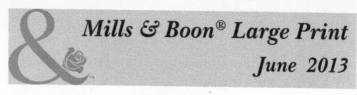

Mills & Boon® Large Print
June 2013

ROMANCE

HISTORICAL

MEDICAL

0513 GEN STD LP

Mills & Boon® Hardback
July 2013

ROMANCE

His Most Exquisite Conquest	Emma Darcy
One Night Heir	Lucy Monroe
His Brand of Passion	Kate Hewitt
The Return of Her Past	Lindsay Armstrong
The Couple who Fooled the World	Maisey Yates
Proof of Their Sin	Dani Collins
In Petrakis's Power	Maggie Cox
A Shadow of Guilt	Abby Green
Once is Never Enough	Mira Lyn Kelly
The Unexpected Wedding Guest	Aimee Carson
A Cowboy To Come Home To	Donna Alward
How to Melt a Frozen Heart	Cara Colter
The Cattleman's Ready-Made Family	Michelle Douglas
Rancher to the Rescue	Jennifer Faye
What the Paparazzi Didn't See	Nicola Marsh
My Boyfriend and Other Enemies	Nikki Logan
The Gift of a Child	Sue MacKay
How to Resist a Heartbreaker	Louisa George

MEDICAL

Dr Dark and Far-Too Delicious	Carol Marinelli
Secrets of a Career Girl	Carol Marinelli
A Date with the Ice Princess	Kate Hardy
The Rebel Who Loved Her	Jennifer Taylor

Mills & Boon® *Large Print*

July 2013

ROMANCE

HISTORICAL

MEDICAL